Back To You

Claude Gress

Copyright © 2023 by Claude Gress

All rights reserved.

No portion of this book may be reproduced in any form without written permission from the publisher or author, except as permitted by U.S. copyright law.

Contents

PROLOGUE 1
CHAPTER 1: The Judgemental Jerk 9
CHAPTER 2: Marry Him 18
CHAPTER 3: Wedding Bells 29
CHAPTER 4: I Do 38
CHAPTER 5: Hubby 46
CHAPTER 6: Business Meeting 55
CHAPTER 7: Dance In The Rain 65
CHAPTER 8: Dad 76
CHAPTER 9: Cousin's Wedding 84
CHAPTER 10: Discipline 92
CHAPTER 11: You Are Mine 100
CHAPTER 12: Confused 108
CHAPTER 13: Jealousy 119
CHAPTER 14: Asshole 133

CHAPTER 15: Dream	143
CHAPTER 16: Heart's Calling	151
CHAPTER 17: Make Me	160
CHAPTER 18: Falling	173
CHAPTER 19: I Missed You	182
CHAPTER 20: Brownie	192
CHAPTER 21: Back To You	207
CHAPTER 22: Misunderstanding	217
CHAPTER 23: I Love You	227
EPILOGUE	239

PROLOGUE

The ten year old boy, sat down on the park's bench; with both his hands, he cupped his cheeks and rested his elbows on his knees.

The setting sun casting a long shadow of his small figure on the ground, the light evening breeze playing with his blonde hair and the deep blue eyes glistening with tears threatening to fall.

Before the tears could fall, he sighed deeply and wiped them away with the back of his palm as a small pout formed on his pink luscious lips.

His stomach growled loudly. Afterall, he had not eaten anything except for a small bowl of soup that he had this morning.

How he wish that a huge plate of food magically appear.

He clutched his stomach and his lips quivered. Hands trembling due to fatigue.

The boy hoped that no one sees him like that and sure there was no one except for the small girl that was watching him from her bedroom's window.

Her house was at a few meters, directly opposite to the small colony's small park.

She was watching him, ever since he sat there. Noticing his every actions even though she was just seven, not old enough to comprehend what exactly was wrong with him.

She has seen that boy a few times but they never met or talked but today before she knew it, her tiny feet carried her out.

Her parents were too busy watching television to notice her going out.

As fast as her tiny feet could carry her, she reached that boy.

For a moment she just stood there, in front of him. When the boy noticed her, he lifted his head and their eyes met.

One stared into those deep blue eyes while the other in those dark brown eyes. The boy was quick to turn his head sideways, he didn't like people to see him being vulnerable.

When he didn't speak, the girl sat beside him quietly. He wanted to tell her to go away but was afraid that his voice will crack and he will break down in front of her.

"What's wrong?", the girl finally spoke after a minute in a soft tone.

The boy turned his head away further at her question.

She poked his shoulder with her index finger. "Say something. Why are you sad? Did someone scold you?"

The boy cleared his throat and with his head still turned sideways he said in a sharp tone, "Nothing happened. Now, go away."

The girl pouted sadly at his answer but got up and giving him one last look, walked away.

He heard her retrieving footsteps and a part of him felt guilty for speaking to her rudely. He felt like going after her and apologize but didn't.

And then all of a sudden, "Boo!"

The boy screamed to see that girl came up to him from the other side and scared the hell out of him.

Seeing the startled expression on his face, the girl started laughing.

The sound of laughter that echoed warmed that boy's heart and for a moment he forgot how hungry he was, he just wanted to laugh along with her or atleast smile as his lips itched to curl up but he bit them instead.

When she finally sobered up, she sat at the same place she was sitting before and this time the boy didn't turn his head sideways but instead was looking at her without making it too obvious.

"So", the girl said, "will you tell me now what happened to you?"

The boy huffed. "You are stubborn, just like my brother", he muttered.

She was scrutinizing his face. And when he didn't speak for a minute she said, "I am waiting."

"Tick...tok...tick...tok", she sang in an annoying tone.

The boy groaned.

"Fine! I am hungry", he admitted.

The girl stopped singing. "Oh."

Then she said innocently after a moment, "Why don't you go back home and eat something?"

The boy shook his head lightly at her innocence and then said in a low, sad voice, "We are poor. We don't have much food at home. There was only little and I told my mother that I am not hungry so that they could eat properly. That's why I am here."

The girl's lips formed an 'O' shape as she understood.

And then she got up. "Wait here."

The boy watched as she ran back towards her house; he didn't know why she wanted him to wait...all he wanted was her to stay a bit longer to give him some company.

He sighed.

But he waited for ten minutes until he saw her emerging from her house but this time, she had a small box in her hand.

As she came closer he realised that it was small pineapple yellow colour tiffin box.

She panted when she stopped in front of him and then sat down again and extended the tiffin box towards him.

"Have this", she said.

"What's that?" He looked at the tiffin box then at her in confusion.

"That's cheese grilled sandwich that I made. That's the only thing I know how to make."

The boy's mouth parted slightly in surprise. "How old are you?"

She grinned. "Seven."

"And you know how to make a sandwich?"

She nodded happily. "Yes, I do. I love cooking but that's the only thing my mom let's me make."

The boy didn't take the tiffin box but just looked at it and then looked ahead.

"Take this", she urged, "I made this for you. Now you have to eat it."

When he still didn't take it, she asked, "You don't like sandwiches?"

To be honest, the boy actually didn't like sandwiches but since he was so hungry and this girl here made it for him, he couldn't say no to her.

He looked at her. "I don't like sandwiches...but...t-thank you. I will eat it.

With hesitation, he slowly took the tiffin box from her hand and opened it to see two pieces of sandwiches inside.

The girl was looking at him carefully as he took a bite of the sandwich. Maybe he was too hungry or maybe the taste of the sandwich was actually addictive that he gobbled it down in a minute.

Chewing the last bite, tears formed in his eyes. He finally could eat something and it was so delicious.

The girl noticed the tears, and her brows knitted together.

"You are crying", she pointed out, "did you not like it?"

He immediately shook his head as a no and swallowing the last bite, he said it aloud, "No. It was delicious. Thank you so much."

The girl grinned happily at his compliment and then leaning forward, she wiped away the single tear that fell on his cheeks with her tiny fingers.

"If you want, you can come again tomorrow and I will make it again for you", she said taking the tiffin box from him.

Before he could reply, she went away.

...

The next day, at the same time, the boy again found himself on that park's bench but this time he was constantly glancing at her house hoping she would come out and yet again give him that sandwich to eat.

He felt embarrassed to ask for it himself, what will she think of him?

So, he waited...and waited...and waited...

And then the door opened and that same girl with the same pineapple yellow colour tiffin box walked out.

She smiled when she saw him and he mirrored her smile.

Her hair was tied in two ponytails that bounced as she ran towards him.

When she stopped in front of him, she held out the tiffin box towards him.

"Grilled cheese sandwich", she said and the boy smiled softly.

And this continued for a week, for a whole week she made the same sandwiches for him and he ate them with the same hunger and love.

Until one day she found herself standing in front of the empty park bench.

He didn't come.

Maybe he is busy and will come later, she thought and sat down on the bench.

She decided to wait for him but...he never came.

Disappointed she got up to leave for her house when she remembered that she once saw his house.

And clutching the tiffin box to her chest she ran to his house.

When she reached there, the first thing she saw was the taxi and the truck standing there and a few people.

Her eyes searched for him and finally they landed on his figure standing beside a woman.

He seemed to be also looking for her and their eyes met.

They both ran towards each other.

"You didn't come today", she said breathlessly.

"I am going", he whispered.

"Where?"

"Houston."

"Why?"

The boy lowered his gaze. "My dad's brother all of a sudden decided to be generous on us. He asked us to move to Houston and promised us a better life."

"So you won't come to Austin again?"

He shook his head. "No."

"Oh", she said and then she remembered something.

"Your sandwich." She gave the box to him.

The boy opened his mouth to speak but was cut off by his father who called him to get in the taxi.

He couldn't say anything as he turned around to leave with the tiffin in his hand.

All of a sudden the girl grabbed his arm and turned him around and then much to his surprise, leaning in, she kissed his cheek.

Yet again he opened his mouth to speak but his father came and gently grabbed his arm and took him away.

Aeryn just stood there and watched him go as he kept glancing back at her. Tears welled up in her eyes.

They never even asked each other's name.

The boy rolled down the taxi's window and stuck his head out and watched the girl as the taxi drove away.

His younger brother nudged his shoulder.

"Everette?", he whispered.

He turned towards his brother. "What, Gareth?"

"Is she your girlfriend?", he whispered making sure no one hears him.

The boy looked out of the window again, watching the girl for the last time.

"Y-yes." His voice shook with emotions threatening to escape.

A tear rolled down his cheek. "Yes, she is."

CHAPTER 1: The Judgemental Jerk

The weather was warm as the sun shone down on the signage board of the restaurant.

The Carmels

It gained popularity recently after being started back a year and a half.

It took Aeryn a lot of part time jobs, some loan from the bank, and her cloud kitchen to save money for the restaurant. Yet it wasn't enough to buy that place in Houston so, she rented it instead.

It had been difficult in the beginning to pay the rent but somehow she managed but now for the past few weeks since the restaurant became the talk of the town, she was finally at peace for she didn't have to worry for the rent anymore.

Just like any other day, Aeryn tied the black apron around her waist and kicked started her day with the hope that this day will bring in more customers today.

As she turned around the corner to enter the kitchen, she was stopped by her overly excited co worker/friend.

"Guess what?!", she shrieked almost jumping up and down.

Aeryn rolled her eyes at her excitement and brushed past her. "There is a sale going on in any of your favorite stores, Harper?"

"No!" She walked upto Aeryn and held her left hand infront of her eyes.

Aeryn looked at her in confusion as she bit her lips and then down at her hand, actually at the small shiny thing on her ring finger.

"Dave proposed you?!", this time Aeryn shrieked.

"Yes!", Harper exclaimed.

"Oh My God!", Aeryn screamed in happiness and engulfed her in a bone crushing hug.

"I am so happy for you! Congratulations!", Aeryn said as they pulled away.

Harper beamed with happiness. "Thank you!"

"You should have taken today a leave and spent some time with Dave."

"It's okay", Harper said, "After all, we are getting so many customers and you need an extra hand."

Aeryn smiled and they both started preparing the dishes together.

...

The morning rolled by and soon it was late in the afternoon when the bell at the door chimed indicating the arrival of a new customer.

Aeryn was too busy making the pasta sauce to see her daughter entering.

It was only when she heard her exclaim, she turned her attention to her.

She saw her daughter hugging Harper tightly after she told her about her engagement.

"Carmel", Aeryn said catching everyone's attention. "What are you doing here?"

Carmel walked closer to Aeryn. "It's Sunday, mama. I was getting bored at home so I came here."

Aeryn placed her hands on her hip. "And how did you reach here?"

"By my bicycle", Carmel said nonchalantly.

"By the way", Carmel said again, "grandma called…she was asking when are we visiting her. I said that mama is busy these days…"

"Oh…I will talk to her later."

Carmel hummed taking a look at the different dishes being cooked in the kitchen.

"Can I go and take the orders?", Carmel asked hopefully.

Aeryn thought for a moment and nodded.

Carmel happily picked up the notepad and a pen and skipped outside to the restaurant to take the orders.

A few minutes later, the bell chimed and a new customer walked in.

Something was different about him because the air around him spoke of power and money.

Dressed in a plain white t-shirt and a pair of jeans, Everette Wilbrose walked in, subtly scanning the interior of the restaurant.

He was alone and he took a seat at the booth in the corner.

He quietly sat down and drummed his fingers against the table. Whenever there is a talk about a new restaurant in the town, Everette Wilbrose has to go there.

Why?

Everyone failed to answer that.

He waited patiently until Carmel decided to take his order.

"Hello", she greeted enthusiastically. "What would you like to have, sir?"

Everette's eyes were focused on the table but on hearing her voice he lifted his head and his mouth parted slightly in surprise and his brows furrowed.

"Aren't you a little too young to be working here?", he questioned her.

Carmel looked down at her legs and eyed herself from head to toe and then twirled around. And then she smiled politely at him.

"No, I seem alright", she said sarcastically. "Do you have any problem?"

Everette's lips pressed into a thin line as he stared at her blankly.

Seeing his expression she chuckled, "I was just kidding. I am just helping my mother; she owns this restaurant."

Everette's expressions became normal at her answer and he smiled softly.

"What's your name, young lady?"

She grinned. "Carmel. And yours?"

He extended his hand for a shake. "I'm Everette. Eve for short."

Carmel shook his hand saying, "That's a rare name."

He just smiled at her and then she asked, "So, Eve...what would you like to order?"

Everette didn't even bother looking at the menu as he said, "Do you guys serve sandwiches?"

Carmel shook her head. "Sorry but we don't serve sandwiches."

He felt disappointed but didn't show it on his face. "So... anything you would like to recommend?"

Carmel's face lit up. "My mama makes the best red sauce pasta. You wanna try some?"

Everette looked at her in adoration. "I would love to."

She grinned widely. "One red sauce pasta coming right up!" With that she turned around and left.

...

"Your red sauce pasta", Carmel said placing down the plate on the table.

"Thank you, Carmel", he said. "Why don't you join me?"

Carmel's eyes widened. "My mother will never let me come here again if she gets to know that I sit and eat her customer's food."

Everette chuckled, "She doesn't need to know and besides...we are friends, right?"

Carmel thought for a minute before running back inside and coming out with an extra plate and culinary.

She sat opposite to Everette and he served some pasta to her before eating himself.

"How old are you, Carmel?"

"Twelve. How old are you?"

"Not much, just thirty."

"You are so old", she remarked.

"Do I really look that old?"

"No...but still, you are old."

"What do you do for a living?", she asked him.

He replied after a pause. "I work in a company."

"Oh...good."

"Are you liking the pasta?", she asked hopefully.

He nodded. "Yes, it's delicious."

She smiled at him. "So...you like sandwiches?"

As a certain memory played in his mind, he couldn't help but smile and say, "I love sandwiches."

Carmel being the talkative one again asked a question. "What's your favourite colour?"

"Pineapple yellow colour."

"Pineapple yellow colour...", she repeated taking a bite of the pasta. "That's very specific. Why this colour?"

"Let's say...it reminds me of something or someone."

"Who?", she asked curiously.

He chuckled. "Someone very special."

"So, you won't tell me." She raised a brow at him.

"Some other day maybe."

"That means we will meet again?"

"Why not? We are friends, right?"

She gave him a toothy grin. "Right."

Slowly the evening started to fall as the restaurant grew quieter; the night is when the main crowd comes in.

As the pasta finished, Carmel got up and collected the dirty utensils to take them back when Everette stopped her.

"Carmel?"

"Yes?"

"Tell your mother that she is very lucky to have you."

"I will!"

Carmel ran back in and keeping away the plates tucked the sleeves of Aeryn's shirt.

"Mama! Mama!", she called.

"Yes, Carmel?"

"There is someone out there who wants to meet you", she told her making Aeryn confused.

"Who's there?"

"Someone. He wants to tell you something. Come on", she urged.

"Carmel, I am busy."

"No", she whined. "You have to come and meet him. Just for a minute, mama. Please!"

Aeryn rolled her eyes. "Ok, I am coming."

"Yes!", Carmel said to herself.

Aeryn wiped her hands with a towel before following Carmel outside to the booth where Everette was patiently sitting and waiting for the bill.

"Eve", Carmel said gaining his attention. "This is my mother."

Aeryn looked at the handsome specimen of a man sitting in her restaurant and couldn't help but glance at him twice.

Carmel introduced them both and Everette slowly stood up, scrutinizing Aeryn's face.

"Is she your daughter?", he asked refering to Carmel who stood there with a grin on her face.

"Yes, she is", Aeryn stated.

"You look so young", Everette blurted out. "And...you have a daughter? How old are you? Twenty?"

"I am not twenty; I am twenty seven!", she said sharply, furious at him for judging her.

"And you, mister, have no right to judge me!", she added pissing off Everette.

"I am not judging you", he spat.

The grin from Carmel's face fell; this isn't what she planned.

Aeryn folded her hands. "So, what else did you mean by 'you look so young and you have a daughter'?!"

"That was just general question!", he argued.

"That didn't sound like it. I demand an apology."

He scoffed. "Not happening. Do you even know who I am?"

"Of course, I do", Aeryn said sarcastically. "You are a Judgemental Jerk!"

Everette's jaw clenched and palm fisted.

"And you are such a stupid girl", he fought back.

Carmel held onto Aeryn's arm.

"Mama", she whispered shouted. "What are doing?"

Aeryn looked at her. "You seriously wanted to make me meet him?!"

Carmel lowered her head. "Sorry."

"Go back inside, Carmel", she said sternly.

And then turned to Everette. "And you can get lost." She then gave him a fake tight smile before grabbing Carmel's hand and dragging her inside.

"Such an asshole", she mumbled.

CHAPTER 2: Marry Him

Aeryn's POV:

"Such and asshole", I mumbled entering the kitchen with Carmel along me.

I made Carmel sit down on a stool as I kneeled in front of her and gently grabbed both her shoulders.

"What was all that about?", I said in a stern tone.

She refused to meet my gaze as she lowered her head.

With my index finger I lifted her chin.

"Carmel", I warned in a gentle tone.

She sighed before explaining her actions. "I was just... I just wanted you both to meet. I thought maybe...you could...erm...date him."

I sighed deeply shaking my head lightly. "You really need to stop playing matchmaker."

"But, mama...", she argued. "He was nice. He was polite."

I was surprised by her words. "Polite? Did you see how he talked to me?"

"But he was very polite to me", she muttered.

"That's because you are just a kid, Carmel."

Tears formed at the corner of her eyes. "I just want you to get a boyfriend and get married. I want you to be happy, mama."

It hurts to see her cry. I slowly cupped her cheek. "I am happy, Carmel. I don't need some man to make me happy. I have you."

There was guilt written all over her face. "But I am the reason no one agrees to date you."

My eyes widened. "Carmel, no..."

"Why don't you tell them I am adopted. That I am not your real daughter."

I lightly smacked her cheeks. "Don't you dare say that ever again."

She lowered her gaze again.

I said softly, "So what if I adopted you? To me, you are my real daughter, Carmel. You are my sunshine."

"And telling everyone you are adopted, won't make a difference. If they want me then they have to accept you too, whether adopted or real", I added.

"I want a father, mama", she whispered.

I froze at her words. "Sorry?"

"My friends, they all have their fathers and I don't have one. I am not saying that you are not enough for me but...I need a father too."

By this time, even I had tears in my eyes and I engulfed Carmel in a warm hug.

"If that's what you want...then I will search for someone", I told her.

She pulled apart and a wide smile formed on her face. "Really?"

With a broken heart, I nodded. "Yes."

Maybe she noticed the sadness on my face because her brows furrowed. "You don't look happy. Don't you want to get married?"

I gave her a sad smile. "I want to...but I am... waiting for someone."

"Who, mama?"

A certain boy with those deep blue eyes appeared in my mind. "My first love."

Carmel gasped. "You first love? And you didn't tell me?!"

"It's not that important. It was a long time back. It's been twenty years since I last saw him. I don't even know where he is."

"You were just seven at that time?"

I nodded. "Yes."

"You have to tell me the whole story now", she demanded.

I ruffled her hair. "Some other time, Carmel."

...

"I am so late. I am so late", I mumbled to myself and grabbed my handbag and quickly wore my shoes.

I need to open the restaurant in the next ten minutes and I have no idea how I woke up so late.

Even though it's my restaurant and it won't be a problem to open it a few minutes late, I like to be punctual.

I already sent Carmel to school, now I need to catch a cab real quick and reach my restuarant.

I walked downstairs from my apartment and onto the footpath when I saw a cab already standing at the other side of the road.

Now, I don't need to wait for it.

I started crossing the road when I realised that I don't remember whether I kept the keys of the restaurant or not.

So, I looked down at my handbag and rummaged through it, still crossing the road.

Oh, it's there.

I sighed in relief and looked up and then suddenly I heard a loud honk of a car and I looked to my left to see a car racing towards me.

A scream left my mouth. That's it. Today is my last day. I am gonna die. Please God, forgive my sins.

I closed my eyes, embracing myself for an impact but it never came.

I slowly opened my eyes to see the car stopped just an inch before me. My knees buckled and I fell down on the road on my butt.

I am alive!

The car's door opened and a man walked out with a worried expression on his face.

He crouched down in front of me. "Are you okay, miss?"

"Ye-ah...I am...okay", I stuttered.

"Thank God", he muttered before he stood up and held out his hand to me.

I looked at his hand and then at him and he gave me a small smile and I reluctantly placed my hand in his and got up.

"Are you sure you are okay? You don't need to go to the hospital, do you?", he asked hurriedly.

I shook my head. "No, I am fine."

I then looked at the other side of the road where the cab was and I saw that it went away.

Great!

"If you want", I head him speak. "I can drop you."

I turned to him. "Sorry?"

He smiled softly. "It seems you were in a hurry and was about to catch a cab and now you are getting even more late so, I can drop you."

"No... it's okay...you don't--"

"Please, I insist."

Since I was so late, I agreed with him and told him my destination.

I sat in the passenger's seat of his Mercedes and took a moment to admire the interior of the car.

"What's your name, miss?", he asked revving the engine and driving away.

"Aeryn. And yours?"

Some unreadable emotion crossed his face but he hid it immediately.

"Gareth. Nice to meet you, Aeryn", he replied.

"Nice to meet you too, Gareth."

The rest of the ride spent in me telling him about my restaurant and stuffs and when he finally dropped me at my restaurant, he told me he would be coming by tonight to have a taste of my dishes.

...

It was late and past the closing time of the restaurant and every other worker had gone so it was only me.

I should close the restaurant but I was waiting for Gareth cause he promised that he will come at night.

Maybe he will be late, that's why I decided to wait for a few more minutes before finally closing it.

I was wiping the counter in the kitchen when the door bell chimed and I happily peeked out to see who came and my mood soured instantly and my face grimaced because the devil himself decided to show up in the form of my landlord, Ronan.

"Aeryn!", I heard him call.

I was supposed to pay the rent the day before yesterday but I still don't have enough money, why doesn't he understand?

I put on a fake smile on my face and walked out.

"Yes, Ronan?"

He had a scowl on his face and his eyes narrowed at me. "Where's the rent?"

"Ronan", I said softly. "I am trying. I need a few more days, that's it."

"You never pay it on time, Aeryn. I don't want any excuses now."

I put on a puppy face and tried convincing him. "Look, Ronan. As you can see that the restaurant is gaining popularity day by day. It won't be long when I'll pay you the rent on time and who knows, maybe I will even buy this place from you."

He scoffed. "You can't pay the rent and you are talking about buying this place."

"I said maybe I will."

As Ronan was about to speak, the door bell chimed again and this time, Gareth walked in.

I gave him a small smile and excusing myself from Ronan, quickly went to him.

"Sorry, I got a bit late", he said.

"No, it's fine. Can you just give me a few minutes, I have to talk to my landlord?"

"Yeah, of course. Take your time. I am sitting there by the way", he said pointing over to a booth and I nodded before going back to Ronan.

"I just need a few more days, Ronan", I said in a low voice.

But Ronan being Ronan, said loudly, "I also need the money, Aeryn. Even I have a family to feed. If you can't afford to pay the rent then you can leave."

I sighed. "Just a few more days?"

"Three days. You have three days not more than that. I don't care where you get the money from." Saying that he angrily left and I sighed in relief.

I went over to Gareth who seemed to be busy on his phone. I took his order and served him within a few minutes and I actually sat down opposite to him and had dinner along with him.

"I am sorry to eavesdrop but", he said. "I can help you in paying the rent. Infact, I can help you buy this whole place."

"That's sweet of you, Gareth but we just met this morning and you are already talking about helping me financially."

He stopped eating and put down his fork. "You didn't understand. What I mean to say is, I will help you financially and in return of which you need to help me."

My brows furrowed. "Help you in what way?"

He took a deep breath as if preparing himself and then he spoke in a low voice. "Well...my brother and I own a company. We are the joint CEOs and recently we need to secure a deal with another company but the problem is, the board of directors of that company wants us to prove them that we are responsible enough for that deal."

My nose scrunched up in confusion. I have no idea what he is trying to say.

He continued, "We actually kinda have a playboy type of an image and in order to fix that and seal that deal one of us need to get married and settle down. I mean, me getting married is out of the question so, that means my brother needs to get married real soon and I am searching for a bride for him."

My mouth slightly parted. "So?"

He ran his fingers through his hair and said nonchalantly, "I want you to marry my brother."

I literally choked on air on hearing his words. I started coughing really badly.

He quickly got up. "Oh my goodness!" He picked up the glass of water and handed it to me and I quickly gulped it down.

"Are you serious?!", I asked as I sobered down.

He chuckled awkwardly. "Unfortunately, yes."

"That's ridiculous, Gareth!"

"I know, I know. But please, try to understand. We need that deal badly and for that we need a bride and you seem perfect to me! And I promise once you sign the papers, all your financially problems will be taken care of", he explained.

"What company do you own?"

"The Wilbrose Enterprises", he stated.

How many more shocks for me today?!

I stood up. "Oh. My. God! Don't tell me you own that multi-billion dollar company?!"

"Aeryn, calm down! And yes, me and my brother own that."

I sat down again. "This is too much, Gareth. I can't do this."

"Just think about it, Aeryn. It's a win-win deal. You help us and we will help you. I promise."

"It's not about that... I...you know half of the people I date don't go on a second date with me because...I have a daughter and having me as their girlfriend will mean pretending to be a father to my daughter."

"I know about your daughter. Her name's Carmel and she is twelve years old and you adopted her when you were fifteen years old and you found her at a garbage dumping area. Right?"

My jaw dropped. "How the hell do you know all that?!"

"I actually...um...dug into your past and took out all that information...", he admitted.

"You stalked me!"

"Look, I am sorry but..."

"That's creepy, Gareth! That's very creepy!"

"Please, at least let me explain."

"Fine!"

"My brother has met your daughter and he is quite fond of her. He is ready to accept her as his daughter. Just marry him, please."

"Show me his picture. How can he meet my daughter without my knowledge?"

He opened his mouth to say something but decided against it. He instead took out his phone and showed me a picture.

"You gotta be kidding me!", I blurted out on seeing his brother's picture ."You want me to marry this judgemental jerk?! And you are saying he is ready to accept my daughter!"

"I heard what happened yesterday and I apologise on his behalf--"

"Apologise on his behalf?!", I snapped at him. "I don't want you to apologise, I want him to apologise!"

"Aeryn, Aeryn. He will apologise...I promise and I really appreciate that you called him a Judgemental Jerk because that was a huge blow to his ego. Wish I was there to see it."

I chuckled at his words. I like this guy.

"So...are you willing to marry him?", he asked hopefully.

"I can't decide on that right now, Gareth but I think you shouldn't be too hopeful about it because my answer is still no."

He sighed and then got up and taking out his wallet he payed the bill. He didn't even ask how much he need to pay, he just payed some amount of money on the table and the amount looked huge.

And then he placed a business card saying, "In case you change your decision. That's my number."

And he walked away leaving me in a deep thought.

CHAPTER 3: Wedding Bells

"Why do you keep feeding me?", the boy asked the little girl, taking a bite of the sandwich.

The girl stopped swinging her legs to and fro from the bench and looked at him.

"Because no one deserves to be hungry", she replied.

The boy smiled and took another bite of the sandwich.

None of them spoke as they sat in a comfortable silence and the boy ate glancing at the little girl once in a while.

A minute later, the sandwich was over and he closed the tiffin box and kept it on the bench.

The girl's attention was focused ahead on the swings and the boy just watched her carefully.

"When I will grow up", he said catching her attention and now she looked at him curiously. "I am going to marry you."

Her face grimaced. "Eww...have you seen your face?"

For a second, his face blanked on hearing her reply and then a small, sad pout formed on his lips and he angrily folded his arms. Huffing, he looked away.

Seeing his reaction, the little girl chuckled. But the boy's expressions didn't change.

So, she poked his cheeks. "Hey?"

No reply.

She again poked his cheek. "Are you angry with me?"

"I was just joking", she said. "Fine, I'll marry you."

That seemed to get a reaction from him as he finally turned his head towards her. "You will?"

She rolled her eyes. "Unfortunately, yes."

A dazzling smile formed on his face. And the little girl giggled.

"But...", she trailed off and he raised his brow.

"How can you be so sure about marrying me?", the little girl asked. "What if I am somewhere else and you are somewhere else?"

The boy smiled softly. "No matter which part of the world I am in, I will always find my way back to you."

And then the smile slowly faded away from his face; the realisation dawned upon him that it wont be long before his family and him will be leaving for Houston and he might never see her again.

He just couldn't bring himself to tell this to her. He just couldn't. At that time, he just wanted to cherish that moment with her.

"When I'll grow up", the girl said with a passion. "I am going to open a restaurant. A huge one. And people will be dying to eat my dishes."

"And I'll help you open it", he added.

"How will you help me?"

He shrugged. "Maybe, you will need some money. Then I will give you the money to help you run your restaurant."

"And in return of that, I will marry you", she said.

He stared into her eyes and whispered, "Yes, you will marry me, brownie."

Her nose scrunched and eyes narrowed. "What? Brownie?"

"Your eyes remind me of brownies, so I am calling you brownie."

"You can't call me that", she said sternly.

"It's a cute name", he argued.

"You like brownies?"

He gave a toothy grin. "I love brownies."

"Fine...you can call me that."

"Thank you, brownie", he said and she giggled._____
_____

Everette's POV:

"Are you fucking crazy, Gareth?!", I yelled.

"How can you randomly ask someone to marry me?! Seriously?!"

He exasperatedly ran his fingers through his hair while sitting on the chair in front of my desk.

I was pacing back and fro when he said, "She is good for you, Eve. She needs our help while we need her."

"Why don't you understand?! I can't marry anyone! Because... because--"

"Because you promised to marry someone else. I know that", he completed my sentence.

"Exactly! You know that I never go back on my words. I can't marry anyone else."

"Come on, Eve! You don't even know where that girl is, how can you marry her?"

"She has to be somewhere", I said desperately.

"It's been twenty years, Eve. You don't even know whether she exists or not."

I snapped at him, "You think I am making up all these stories?! You think she never existed and I was just hallucinating her? You saw her too, didn't you?"

"Twenty years... that's a long time..."

"She is there and I will find her and marry her only. That's final!"

He angrily got up. "Use your fucking brain, Everette! We need this deal and for that you have to get married! We can't lose this deal just because you are waiting for someone whose name you don't even know!"

Gareth is usually a calm person, he hardly loses his cool and this really surprised me.

Both of us became silent and had a staring competition and Gareth was the one to break it first.

"Sorry", he muttered and I rolled my eyes. "But you are marrying Aeryn."

I felt like throwing him off from my office window which was at the 50th floor.

"And you only said that you became quite fond of her daughter Carmel."

"That doesn't mean I'll marry her."

He walked upto me and grabbed both my shoulders and dragging me made me sit in my swivel chair.

"Now, listen to me", he said keeping both his hands on the side of the chair trapping me making sure I don't run away.

"You marry Aeryn, we secure this deal meanwhile I will help you find this girl, okay?", he said.

"What if I marry Aeryn and then I find that girl?"

"Then, you and Aeryn will get a divorce and I, myself will make you marry that girl. I promise."

"What if we don't find that girl?"

He smirked. "If within three months, we don't find that girl then...you are going to make this marriage between Aeryn and you, work. You will accept Aeryn as your wife and treat her like a queen and you will forget about that girl. Okay?"

My jaw clenched. "This is absurd."

"This is the deal, brother. You have to agree to it. Okay?"

"No--"

He cut me off by patting my cheek. "Good boy."

"Fuck off", I seethed.

He just grinned and moved back and said, "And call Aeryn and apologize to her saying you are willing to marry her."

I scoffed. "Not happening. It was her mistake."

"Oh, for God's sake, keep your ego aside for a moment and apologize to her."

"I am not apologising to her!"

"Oh, you will", with that he turned around and moved towards the door. "I have a meeting in five minutes, by the time it ends I am hoping to hear a good news. Bye!"

I sighed in frustration and held my face in my hands.

Aargh!

Three minutes later, my phone's notifications started going off one after the other.

Who the fuck died now?!

I picked it up to see that Gareth tweeted something and tagged me in it.

"So excited to see my brother @everetteWilbrose get married in a few days! #weddingbellsintheair"

(A/N: Everette be like, "Abey saale!".)

The fuck!

She hasn't even agreed to marry me and he already tweeted about it.

Are you fucking crazy, Gareth!

I already started getting so many 'congratulations' messages.

What did you do, Gareth?!

And then my phone rang: Mother

Great!

I picked up the call and said in the sweetest tone possible. "Yes, mother?"

"You are getting married and you didn't even bother to tell me?!", she shrieked.

"Mother--"

"No, no, no! When were you going to tell me? On the wedding day? I am sure you were not even planning on inviting me!"

I tried making her understand. "Of course you are invited, mother. But right now, I am not sure if this marriage will take place or not."

"What do you mean? I already told all my friends about it!"

I face slammed myself. "Mother, it's been only a few minutes since Gareth tweeted and you told all your friends already?"

"Can you blame me? I was so excited and plus it's 2021, how long does it take to send a message to all your friends?"

"Oh, mother..."

"I don't wanna hear your drama now. And who is the girl you are marrying?"

"Umm...her name is...Aeryn. She owns a restaurant."

"And?"

"And...and...she has a daughter..."

"O-kay...so, what about that her daughter's father?"

"Mother, she is adopted. Aeryn adopted when she herself was fifteen. And...I am ready to be her father."

"Aww...she is so kind! And I am so proud of you, son."

"Thanks, mother."

"So, when is the wedding?"

I told her a random day. "This Sunday."

"Yay! Then I will see you on Saturday! Bye!"

"Mother--" But the call ended.

And now how to tell her that all this is fake and...I don't even know whether she will agree to marry me or not.

I somehow managed to get Aeryn's personal number and dialled it.

A few rings later, she picked up. "Hello?"

I cleared my throat. "Is this Aeryn Reynolds?"

"Yes. And who is this?"

"Everette Wilbrose."

She went silent for a minute and then she spoke. "What do you want, Mr Wilbrose?"

"I...umm...wanted to *clears throat* apologise for my behavior that day."

I heard her sigh. "Fortunately, your apology has been accepted. Now if you may excuse me, I am very busy at the moment."

She was about to hang up but I said, "No, Aeryn! Wait!"

"Yes, Mr Wilbrose?", She said impatiently.

"There is one more thing..."

"I am listening."

"I need you to marry me. My brother talked to you about it the other day."

"Yes, he did."

"And... what's your answer? Are you accepting it?"

"If you apologise to me in a much better way, I might accept your proposal. Oh, and a bouquet of white roses may help you. Tonight, 10 pm at my restaurant. See you later, Mr Wilbrose. Thank you."

And she hung up the call.

The nerve of that girl!

I massaged my temples for a few seconds before opening the bottom drawer in my desk and taking out the pineapple yellow colour tiffin box.

The colour was fading and I traced my finger over it. "Where are you my little brownie?"

CHAPTER 4: I Do

Aeryn's POV:

"I am so scared, Harper", I said in a frightful tone.

Harper rubbed my back gently. "Nothing will happen. He is not going to eat you up."

After I told Everette Wilbrose to apologise to me in a better way or else I won't be accepting his offer, I am freaking out.

It was so easy to say all that over a call but what if he actually show up?!

Wait a minute.

Why am I scared of him?

He should be the one to be scared by me.

I even know some tricks of martial arts. It won't be difficult to take him down.

Let him come tonight.

...

Once again it was late and everyone has went home for my restaurant closes at 9:30 pm everyday.

And once again I was cleaning the kitchen counter when the doorbell chimed and as expected, Everette Wilbrose walked in.

I washed my hands and walked outside and I almost chuckled to see a bouquet of white roses in his hand and his jaw was clenched. He wore a black shirt and a pair of jeans and I had to stop myself from drooling at him.

When our eyes met, I smiled cheekily and walked closer. And he shoved the bouquet in my hands.

"Quite rude but I will let it pass", I remarked.

"Anything you would like to have, Mr Wilbrose?", I asked.

"No", he gritted.

"Okay. Take a seat, Mr Wilbrose."

He rolled his eyes and walking past me, sat in a booth and I took a seat opposite to him after keeping away the bouquet.

Neither of us spoke at first and I drummed my fingers against the table.

"Stop drumming your fingers", he snapped.

"Is it irritating you?", I questioned in a saccharine tone.

"Yes."

I stopped drumming my fingers and gave him a toothy grin after which I once again started drumming them, a bit louder and faster this time.

"Fucking stop it!", he seethed.

I stopped drumming them. "Well, you are not saying anything so I was getting bored."

"Are you going to marry me or not?", he spoke immediately.

"Mmm...nice question..."

He slammed his fist on the table making me flinch. "I don't have that much time. Just answer the damn question!"

"Okay, okay. If you are that desperate then I'll marry you."

His jaw clenched even more but he didn't say anything.

"You know your brother is nicer than you", I stated.

His eyes narrowed at me. "Then why don't you go marry him."

"Oh, I would love to but too sad he is not available. He said he doesn't want to get married so soon", I drawled.

His hand that was resting on the table slowly clenched into a fist.

"You seem bothered, Mr Wilbrose. Are you alright?", I drawled again.

"Don't call me that", he gritted.

"Why? You have a problem with being called by your last name, Mr Wilbrose?"

"You are my fiance; call me by my first name."

"Fiance?" I then lifted my left hand. "I don't see an engagement ring."

When I said that, he dig his hands in his pocket and took out a velvet, black box.

And he slid that box to me. "Help yourself."

"Very funny. Unless and until you make me wear it, I am not wearing it."

He mumbled something underneath his breath and then taking the box opened it, revealing a diamond ring.

Before I knew it, he roughly grabbed my left hand and slid that ring down my ring finger within a second.

"It wasn't that difficult, was it?", I said much to his annoyance.

"Don't expect this marriage to ever work between us", he stated.

"I never said I am expecting this to work. I am agreeing to marry you just for my restaurant and my daughter. Nothing else."

"Judgemental Jerk", I muttered underneath my breath but he heard it.

"What do you think of yourself?", he said.

"What do you think of yourself?", I mocked referring to him and his eyes narrowed even more and his lips pressed into a thin line.

"I am making such a huge mistake by marrying you", he mumbled to himself and thankfully I heard it.

"That you are", I told him much to his surprise.

He got up immediately and made his way towards the door when I said, "Leaving so soon? I thought you will stay a little longer and we would enjoy."

I moved closer to him and he turned towards me.

And then standing on tip toes I pulled both his cheeks in a puerile way. "Aww...bye-bye, Everette. I'll miss you."

He took a deep breath trying to control his rage and I was quite impressed by his self-control.

He didn't say anything and just removed my hands from his cheeks and turned to leave.

As his figure moved out the door I shouted, "Goodnight!"

And of course, I didn't get a reply.

...

"Oh My God! Oh My God! I am so nervous!"

"For the hundreth time, Harper, this is my wedding day not yours", I told her. I have no idea why she is freaking out.

"I know, I know! But I still can't believe you are marrying Everette Wilbrose! He is so handsome! And I just saw him standing there today and damn! He is wearing a tuxedo and hotness is oozing out of him. You are so lucky!"

"That's enough! Stop praising him and tell me how am I looking?"

"Oh, my dear friend. You are looking absolutely gorgeous. Gracefulness is oozing out of you and it sure will make everyone's jaws drop", she said dramatically.

I grinned. "Thank you, thank you."

"Yes, mama; you are looking beautiful. Everette is going to be spellbound", Carmel said making us acknowledge her presence.

"And I am so happy you are marrying him", she said dreamily, twirling around. "He is perfect for you."

"Yeah... yeah..."

Later my parents came and complimented me saying how happy they are and all that. I didn't tell them the real reason behind the marriage; I made up a fake story and told them that. Thankfully, they believed it.

...

I hooked my arm with my dad before we took our position before the church gate.

This is it. I am getting married.

The music started playing and the door opened and dad and I started walking down aisle.

It was small ceremony that included only the family members and close relatives.

Everette was standing there in a black tuxedo as Harper told me and besides him was Gareth standing as the best man. I never knew they were so close to each other.

Everette had a poker face and even when our eyes met, I couldn't make out a single emotion on his face.

Reaching Everette, dad gave my hand to him as his cold fingers wrapped around my hand and he made me stand opposite to him.

The ceremony started and the priest started speaking to which I didn't pay any attention to. I completely zoned out.

I was lost in my thoughts when I heard someone clear his throat and I felt a squeeze on my hand.

I lifted my gaze and saw that the priest had asked me something.

"Sorry", I mumbled and the priest repeated his words.

"Do you, Aeryn Reynolds, take Everette Wilbrose to be your lawfully wedded husband?"

I took a deep breath. "I do."

"I now pronounce you husband and wife. You may now kiss the bride."

And the colour drained from my face. I am not going to kiss him; he can go kiss his ass.

Everette took a step closer and lifted my veil and stared into my eyes intensely.

He cupped both my cheeks and leaned closer and then I felt his soft pair of lips at the corner of my mouth. And he immediately stepped back as the crowd cheered.

That was close.

Later when the ceremony got over and everything was done, I said goodbye to everyone.

At last I said to Carmel, "Are you sure you will be fine?"

"Yes, mama. I will be enjoying with grandma and grandpa while you enjoy your honeymoon in Australia." She winked at the last part of sentence.

I glared at her but she only chuckled and I then kissed her forehead before she pushed me towards Everette.

I said goodbye to everyone one last time before sitting inside the car with Everette.

"This is not a honeymoon", I heard him speak as the car moved.

I rolled my eyes. "I know."

"This is a business trip, I hope you know that", he said again.

"Yes, yes! I know that. You don't need to keep rubbing that in my face", I said exasperatedly.

He looked at me for a moment before looking out of the window.

"What about my restuarant's rent?", I asked.

"Taken care of. I bought that place. You don't need to worry about the rent anymore", he spoke.

"Oh...thank you", I whispered and he hummed in response.

I sighed deeply; I have no idea how I am going to spend a week with him in Australia.

CHAPTER 5: Hubby

Everette's POV:

I tapped her shoulder. "Aeryn?"

"Aeryn, wake up." I again tapped her shoulder and she groaned.

"You can sleep in the hotel but get up now. We don't have all day to spend in the jet."

Instead of waking up, she slapped away my hand.

It's hardly been a day since we got married and she is already getting on my nerves.

"You have left me with no choice", I muttered and then picked her up in my arms in bridal style. And she automatically snuggled into my neck.

The moment she snuggled into my neck I felt weird. A good type of weird and I lightly shook my head trying to brush it off.

With her in my arms I carefully climbed down the steps of the jet. When I glanced at her I saw that one of her eyes was open and she was peaking at me.

"You were awake all this time, huh?"

She rolled her eyes. "Obviously."

My jaw clenched. "You did this to irritate me?"

She grinned and nodded.

"Get down, immediately", I ordered.

"No", she whined.

"Get down, Aeryn or I am going to throw you on the floor." I loosened my grip on her body but she tightly wrapped her arms around my neck.

"No! Don't throw me! You have to carry me now like this."

We were already getting late so giving her one last glare I carried her to the car. The driver greeted me and opened the door and with her in my arm, I slipped in.

Once inside, she still didn't make an effort to move.

"Get off now", I said.

She shook her head. "No."

"Aeryn", I warned her. "Get off my lap."

"Not until we reach the hotel", she said.

And I groaned in frustration knowing she is not going to listen to me.

So, with her still sitting in my lap, I took out my phone and started answering a few emails while she looked out of the window as the car moved.

All of a sudden, she started poking my cheek.

"What now?", I spat.

"And don't touch me", I muttered afraid if she touches me I will feel weird again but I guess she didn't hear it.

"Stop using your phone and enjoy the scenery after all we are in Sydney."

"I have already visited Sydney before. And now don't disturb me", I told her dryly.

I focused my attention back on my phone and from the corner of my eyes saw her rolling her eyes.

I feel like strangling Gareth for making me marry her.

...

"The view from here is so beautiful!", she exclaimed looking out of the glass wall of our presidential suit.

After getting freshened up, I took out my laptop and settled down on the coffee table in the room and started working.

"Come on, Everette", she said standing in front of me. "Let's go somewhere!"

I had my eyes focused on the laptop and said, "I am busy, Aeryn."

"No", she whined. "I want to go somewhere!"

"I said I am busy", I said a bit loudly.

"And I said I want to go somewhere."

All of a sudden, she shut my laptop and my head jerked up to her as I glared at her. "What the fuck, Aeryn?!"

She smiled innocently. "Let's go somewhere."

I got up angrily. "Don't you understand simple english? I told you I am busy!"

She frowned. "I am getting bored here."

"That's not my problem. Go, entertain yourself; I don't care!"

She walked closer to me and grabbed my forearm. "Come on, if you won't work a few hours, it won't hurt."

I yanked myself out of her grip. "Don't touch me!"

She scowled. "What are you? A president?"

"Just don't touch me."

"You know what?" She walked even closer. "I will touch you."

Saying that she shoved my shoulder. "See. I touched you."

"Aeryn", I warned.

She then shoved my other shoulder. "I touched you again."

She was about to touch me again but I caught her wrist tightly. "Enough!"

In a moment she turned her hand and moving backwards twisted my arm and broke free of my hold.

I groaned rubbing my arm and she grinned. "For your kind information, I know some tricks of martial arts so you better be careful about hurting me."

My eyes widened a little in surprise but I quickly covered it. I really need to be careful now.

"Now, Mr Wilbrose", she said. "Can we go out now?"

"No", I stated and she narrowed her eyes.

I sat down again and opened my laptop and started working.

The next few seconds she was silent but then she spoke, "Can't you take me out? I am your wife."

I chuckled humorlessly. "Wife? Seriously, Aeryn?"

I continued, "I already told you that this marriage is only on paper. Don't expect it to work, okay?"

Her brows knitted together. "You don't consider me your wife?"

"No", I said in a heartbeat.

She went over to the bed and sat at the edge of it. "So...you won't mind if I go out and find someone else to explore the place with?"

"Definitely not. You are free to do whatever you want."

"Very well! Then, I am going!" She got up excitedly and without even bothering about her dress or makeup, grabbed her handbag and walked to the door.

"Ba-bye!" She waved her hand.

I waved back. "Bye, Aeryn! Enjoy!"

And she went away. Peace. Finally.

I dialled my bodyguard's number.

"Keep an eye on her. Make sure she is safe", I told him before hanging up.

.

.

It has been an hour since she left and I couldn't be more grateful for it.

My phone buzzed and a notification went off. I picked it up to see a message from Aeryn.

I opened it and she had sent me a picture, the picture download and I saw that she was standing in front of the Sydney Opera House but the main thing was, she was not alone.

There was a man with her, green eyes, clean shaved face. He had his arm wrapped around her shoulder while they both smiled for a picture. She did find someone to explore with. Good for her.

I kept my phone aside and continued with my work.

Half an hour later, I again received a picture from her. This time it was a selfie and they both had ice cream in their hands.

I rolled my eyes and again kept my phone aside continuing with my work.

And again half an hour later, I received yet another picture. She was still with that man in a church and she wrote under it: Enjoying with Sam.

Yes, yes, enjoy with Sam or whoever the hell he is. I don't care.

Five minutes later...*sighs*...I again received a picture, I wasn't going to download it but I did it anyway and the moment I saw the picture, my grip on the phone tightened.

It was a selfie and they both were in a cafe, sitting too close for my liking and the thing that made my blood boil was their faces that were inches apart and they both had pouted their lips and were about to kiss.

The fuck!

I quickly dialled my bodyguard's number and asked him to tell me her location.

As soon as I got her location, I ran down to the lobby and went outside where there was a car already waiting for me and I climbed in telling the driver the location.

The cafe was not far away and I reached there in fifteen minutes. The cafe was near the sea and they were sitting outside on a table, chatting and laughing with each other with their backs towards me.

That's enough exploration for today.

I marched towards them and grabbing Aeryn's chair, I dragged it back so that she was facing me.

Her eyes widened in shock and before she could open her mouth, I bent down and grabbing her legs, thew her over my shoulder not caring about the public who were staring at us.

She punched my back. "Put me down!"

"We are going back to the hotel."

I put her inside the car and then slipped in beside her.

The whole ride back to the hotel she had her arms folded and kept grumbling to herself while throwing daggers towards me.

As we reached the hotel, I grabbed her hand and dragged her upto our room.

"What the hell is your problem?!", she shouted once we were inside the room.

"Why? I ruined your perfect date?", I mocked her.

She folded her hand and rolled her eyes. "Yeah...you did. I was enjoying a lot. He was so much better than you."

"Locking lips in the name of enjoyment, huh?"

"Oh, yeah...his lips were so soft and sweet...", she drawled.

My jaw clenched. "I don't need the details."

"And that's enough exploration for today", I told her dryly.

"Who are you to decide that?"

My head snapped to her. "Who am I? Your husband; that's what I am."

"Husband? Seriously Everette?", she mocked. "I told you this marriage was on papers only. Don't expect it to work, okay?"

My palm folded into a fist and I cleared my throat. "I take my words back."

She grinned. "So, do you consider me as your wife?"

I took a deep breath. "Yes, I do. Happy?"

"Very."

She then moved past me into the room but I grabbed her hand and brought her in front of me.

"But that also means I am your husband."

She gave me a salute. "Of course, hubby." And winking at me she went inside.

...

During night, I changed my clothes and wore a pair of sweatpants leaving my upper body uncovered.

When I walked into the room, Aeryn was standing in a corner scrolling through her phone. She glanced at me and immediately lowered her gaze, a tint of pink appearing on her cheeks.

"We can share the bed; it's large enough", I said gaining her attention. "Or if you are uncomfortable, I can take the couch."

She scratched the back of her neck. "Oh, umm...we can...share the bed."

I shrugged my shoulders and layed down on one side, with my back towards her.

Few seconds later, she switched off the lights and I felt the bed dip as she layed down.

A minute passed by when I heard her clearing her throat.

"Everette?", she whispered.

"Hmm?"

She again cleared her throat. "I didn't kiss him. That was just to irritate you."

"Go to sleep, Aeryn", I whispered and she mumbled goodnight.

With my eyes still closed, a smiled formed on my face. Of course, she didn't kiss him.

And sighing in relief, I drifted off to sleep.

CHAPTER 6: Business Meeting

Aeryn's POV:

"Aeryn."

"Aeryn."

"Aeryn", the voice said a bit louder this time.

Why does everyone has to ruin my beauty sleep?

I slowly opened my eyes and came face to face with Everette who was glaring at me, his face showed signs of displeasure.

"I just woke up. What did I do now?", I questioned.

His lips were pressed into a thin line and gestured down to his hand. I looked down and saw I was holding onto his hand tightly as if my life was dependent on it.

A blush crept up my neck and I immediately removed my hand feeling embarrassed.

Rolling his eyes, he got up and went inside the washroom.

What a start to the morning!

Yawning, I got up and firstly messaged Harper inquiring about the restaurant as I left it in her care.

I spent the next fifteen minutes scrolling through the phone. The door of the washroom opened and Everette stepped out dressed in a black suit.

"Are you going somewhere?"

He was standing infront of the mirror combing his hair, he glanced at me through the mirror. "Yes. Business meeting."

"Oh. Good. Enjoy there", I said sarcastically.

One side of his lips curled up into a smirk. "You are coming with me."

"What?!"

"You are coming with me to the meeting. I am not leaving you here. God knows what you will do."

I got and placed both my hands on my hip. "I am not a kid. I can take care of myself. I am not going to some boring meeting with you."

He put down the comb and came closer to me. His cologne invaded my mind. Mmm... that's a nice cologne.

"Get ready, Aeryn. We will get late. I won't repeat myself."

"I am not going with you. And even I won't repeat myself."

He turned away from me and muttered, "Fine. Don't come with me. I was thinking of exploring a few places after the meeting with you."

"Give me twenty minutes", I mumbled walking past him and into the washroom.

...

I opened my hair letting it fall over my shoulder and checked myself in the mirror.

Grabbing my handbag I went out in the living room where he was waiting for me. He looked up from his phone and scanned me for a second before subtly nodding and asked me to follow him.

A car was waiting for us outside and we both slipped in as the car moved.

Half an hour later, the car stopped infront of a skyscraper.

Hamilton Enterprises.

Once Everette got out, he held out his hand for me to hold and I placed my hand in his. His warm fingers intertwining with mine.

"We are supposed to act like real couples", he whispered in my ear dragging me along with him.

"Understood."

We walked inside the building and there was a man waiting for us at the reception. On seeing us he quickly came forward.

"Welcome, Mr and Mrs Wilbrose", he greeted. "I am Benjamin Hans, Mr Hamilton's personal assistant."

He extended his hand and Everette shook his hand, next he turned to me and I extended my hand too but instead he took it gently and lightly kissed my knuckles.

I smiled shyly at him and he smiled back before telling us to follow him.

Everette all of a sudden, pulled me closer and wrapped his hand tightly around my waist.

I could do nothing but play along with him.

We followed Benjamin into the elevator and he pressed the 20th floors button.

The elevator opened onto the 20th floor and we got out. Near the receptionist's table, another man was waiting for us and he smiled on seeing us stepped forward while Benjamin went and stood beside him.

Everette smiled too and they both shook their hands.

"Hello, Mr Hamilton", Everette greeted. He then pulled me even more closer. "And this is my lovely wife, Aeryn."

Lovely wife my foot!

Mr Hamilton smiled politely. "Nice to meet you, Mrs Wilbrose."

I smiled back. "Nice to meet you too, Mr Hamilton."

Mr Hamilton opened his mouth to speak but was cut off by someone's screaming.

He literally face slammed himself while shaking his head.

The screaming got louder and closer and we looked behind him to see a little boy being chased by two little girls. They all looked the same age. Around five.

The boy came running towards us and hid behind Mr Hamilton.

"Uncle, uncle!", he said in a hurry. And then pointed towards the girls. "They both are beating me."

Sighing, Mr Hamilton picked him up in his arms and then turned towards the girls. "Raven and Addison. Why are you both troubling him?"

"Dad", one of the girl said but was cut off by the other.

"Uncle, he broke our car!", she complained and it was then I noticed that the boy and the girl who addressed Mr Hamilton as uncle, they both were twins.

"Why did you break their cars?", Mr Hamilton asked the boy in a stern tone.

He shook his head innocently. "I didn't."

"He did!", both the girls said.

"Okay, kids! You all go inside right now, I will deal with you all later", he told and then turned towards us.

He smiled sheepishly. "I am sorry about about them." Then he pointed towards the twins. "They are my best mate/wife's brother's kids and she is my daughter. My wife is eight months pregnant and my best mate is busy at the moment while his wife is out of town, so I have the responsibility to look after them."

The children were still present there, they refused to go inside.

"No problem, Mr Hamilton", Everette said.

"Yes, they are adorable", I added.

Mr Hamilton chuckled. "Adorable? They are packet full of trouble. They are only adorable for the first few minutes after that they eat up your head."

The kids didn't look happy with the way they were introduced. The twin girl tugged on his legs. "Uncle, I want to introduce myself."

"Me too!", the boy said.

"Me too!", Mr Hamilton's daughter said.

"Fine", he mumbled before he picked the twin girl in his other arm.

"Hi! My name is Rafe and I am five years old", the boy introduced himself.

"And I am mom's favourite", he added making me chuckle.

"Hi! My name is Addison and I am also five years old. And I am both dad and mom's favourite", the girl said.

Mr Hamilton shook his head exasperatedly. "You are not supposed to say that in an introduction."

Both Everette and I, laughed softly.

He then put both of them down and took his daughter in his arms.

"Hi! My name is Raven and I am six years old", his daughter said and put her down.

I crouched down said, "Hi! My name is Aeryn and I am twenty seven years old."

"You are so old", Rafe said.

"Rafe! You don't say that", Mr Hamilton scolded him.

"Oh, it's fine, Mr Hamilton", I said and got up. "Do you mind if I play with them while you have your meeting?"

"Are you sure? Because they might look adorable but their actions are not", he warned.

"It's okay. I love kids."

He looked worried but smiled eventually and nodded.

His assistant, Benjamin took me and the kids to a room and Everette and Mr Hamilton left for their meeting.

The room was quite large and the walls were painted with the princesses and cartoons. There was a door that led to a small washroom and another door that led to a small kitchen. The floor was littered with different toys, a small slide and various other things.

"I hope you will be okay with them", Benjamin said.

"Yes, of course."

Nodding he left.

There was a small couch and I went and sat there and watched them play with each other.

Initially, they were playing peacefully. The three of them were having a car race.

Raven lost the race but Addison and Rafe's cars had a tie.

"I won!", Rafe exclaimed happily.

Addison got up and smacked his head. "No, I won."

Rafe shoved her. "No, I won!"

Addison pouted angrily and screamed, "I won! You didn't!"

Before they start beating each other, I instantly got up and went over to them.

"Umm...why don't you both again have a race and then decide", I advised them and the three of them looked at me curiously.

"Good idea, Aarin", Addison spoke.

"Umm... it's Aeryn not Aarin", I corrected her.

"Aarin", she tried to say Aeryn but couldn't pronounce it.

"Nevermind", I said. "You can call me anything."

She nodded and turned to her brother. "Let's race again."

I sighed when they start to have another race and I went and sat on the couch again.

I didn't pay much attention to them as I was busy using my phone, scrolling through Instagram.

I don't know why but that boy with those deep blue eyes appeared in my mind and I sighed. I don't know where he is. Is he okay?

Tears started to form in my eyes and I quickly blinked them away and stopped thinking about him.

If destiny wants, I will meet him again someday.

Besides that, I can't do anything.

Time passed and I was still sitting in the same place but now I had my head in my hands cause it started paining.

Why?

Because for the last fifteen minutes these three are running around the room continuously and they were shouting too. Non stop.

I tried to stop them but they threatened to beat me and throw me out of the room. Seriously?

Now I understand why Mr Hamilton was so worried about me.

All of a sudden, the noise reduced and I lifted my head and saw that the girls were now playing with their Barbie dolls.

Rafe walked to me and pointed towards my phone. "I want that."

"Why don't you go and play with your sisters?"

"No! I want the phone!"

I gripped the phone tightly. "I am not giving it to you."

He shouted. "Phone!"

I shook my head and he turned around and ran to the kitchen. He came back a second later with a knife in his hand.

The hell!

He pointed the knife towards me. "Phone!"

Oh my goodness!

I unlocked my phone and promptly handed it to him. He dropped the knife and I picked it up.

He grinned and took the phone from my hand and settled on the couch beside me.

That five year old kid opened You Tube, went to the search bar, selected the option of voice search and put on a video that was showing different toy cars in it.

My jaw dropped.

Before I could react, both Addison and Raven came to me.

"Aarin, I am hungry", Addison said.

"Me too", Raven added.

"Uh...okay...what do you want to eat?"

"Apple!", they both said together.

O-kay...

I went into that small kitchen and found some apples there. I cut them into small pieces and taking a fork with me, went outside.

Once settled on the couch, both the girls sat on the floor and asked me to feed them.

So, that's what I did.

I fed them the apple and they both looked so adorable while eating.

Half way through feeding them, I felt someone's gaze on me.

I lifted my head and looked towards the door where I found Everette leaning against the doorway, looking at me with a small smile on his face.

CHAPTER 7: Dance In The Rain

Aeryn's POV:

I fed them the apple and they both looked so adorable while eating.

Half way through feeding them, I felt someone's gaze on me.

I lifted my head and looked towards the door where I found Everette leaning against the doorway, looking at me with a small smile on his face.

Our eyes met and he looked startled for a moment before he cleared his throat and the smile disappeared from his face.

"The meeting is over. We are leaving", he announced.

I nodded and finished feeding the girls. Just then Mr Hamilton walked in and his brows furrowed when he saw Rafe was using my phone.

"Rafe", he said. "Whose phone are you using?"

Rafe looked up and then innocently pointed towards me.

"Mrs Wilbrose", he addressed me. "You shouldn't have given him the phone."

"I wasn't going to give him but...he threatened me with a knife", I admitted sheepishly.

Mr Hamilton's eyes widened and he walked closer to Rafe and snatched my phone from him and handed it to me.

"Say sorry to her", he ordered him.

Rafe pouted angrily and refused to apologise; Mr Hamilton glared at him.

"Sorry", he said.

I ruffled his hair. "It's okay. But don't threaten anyone with a knife again."

He just glared at me and went over to his sisters.

Mr Hamilton again apologised to me personally and I told him to brush it off.

We all got up to leave but stopped when someone entered the room.

"Kids, I am back!", the person said and the children ran to him.

He crouched down and the children went and hugged him.

Mr Hamilton went to him and he got up.

Mr Hamilton placed his hand around hi shoulder and introduced him. "Mr and Mrs Wilbrose, this is my best mate and the captain of the Australian Cricket Team, Nelson Andrews."

Everette and I shook his hand, introducing ourselves.

Mr Andrews turned to the kids and said, "Let's go everyone!"

He picked up the girls in his arms as Rafe followed him out.

Mr Hamilton sighed deeply in relief and Everette and I said our goodbyes.

...

I did visit Sydney Opera House yesterday but that was in the afternoon. It looks even more beautiful in the evening. And I was really happy that Everette brought me here.

We spent the whole evening visiting different places and at last, we stopped by Sydney Opera House.

He has already removed the coat and has rolled up the sleeves of his white shirt making him look more hot.

Anyway...

I wanted to have a picture with Everette with the Sydney Opera House in the background.

I looked around and spotted a couple and I ran to them and giving them my phone, requested them to click my picture.

They nodded happily and I ran back to Everette and held his hand.

"Smile", I said pointing towards the phone.

I expected him to protest but he didn't, instead he wrapped his hand around my waist, pulling me closer and we both smiled for the picture.

The couple came to us after clicking the picture and handing the phone to me they complimented, "You both look great together. Made for each other."

I smiled politely at them as my cheeks turned red; I didn't even look at Everette to see his reaction.

We were walking away when I said, "I am hungry."

"I want food", I continued to say.

"Something delicious. I am so hungry--"

"I already heard you", he cut me off boorishly.

I scowled at him. "You don't need to be rude."

Ignoring my statement he asked, "What do you want to eat?"

My mood lifted. "Chinese!"

...

We took a seat at the table set at the rooftop of the restuarant from where the view was amazing; you could see the sea at the distance and the Sydney Opera House.

I was still admiring the view when someone cleared his throat. I turned my attention to Everette and found a waiter standing there.

He was so cute. Like really. He was smiling and had dimples on his cheeks.

He introduced himself. "I'm Alberto and I will be your waiter tonight."

I smiled in response and he handed us the menu, his attention mainly on me.

He went away giving us time to decide the dishes.

I decided what I wanted to eat and closed the menu and looked at Everette who also seemed to have decided what he wanted to eat.

He called for Alberto and he was here within a second.

"Did you decide what you want to have?", he directed his question to me, with that adorable smile still plastered on his face.

I gave him my order and he took Everette's too after which he went away.

I sighed and focused my attention to Everette who was already scrutinizing my face.

"So...umm...you are a self-made billionaire?", I said in a failed attempt to start a conservation.

"Yes", he said in a monotone. "Gareth and I started the company from scratch ten years back. We worked day and night to reach here."

"Oh", I whispered. He doesn't seem to be much interested in a conversation considering the way he spoke.

I sighed and again looked at the view. Why am I sighing so much?

All I ever wanted was to start my own restuarant and marry my first love. But destiny seems to have other plans.

I never wanted to marry a billionaire, I just wanted to marry that boy with those deep blue eyes. Whenever I think about him it bring tears to my eyes. I don't know where he is or how he is or...or is he even alive?

My thoughts were interrupted by the arrival of our food. Alberto placed our food on the table and giving me one last smile, went away.

I moaned taking a bite of the chilli garlic noodles and Everette gave me a weird look.

I glared at him. "What?"

He shook his head. "Nothing."

I took another bite of the noodles and moaned again and he scowled at me. "Stop moaning."

"What? It's delicious."

"Stop it or else I will give you a better reason to moan."

I almost choked at his words and my cheeks burnt with embarrassment.

I stopped moaning and quietly ate my noodles.

He smirked at my reaction and resumed eating.

Jerk!

We finished our food in silence and the plate were taken away by Alberto and Everette handed him his credit card.

He returned and handed Everette his card back he again smiled at me and said. "Goodbye. Have a nice evening."

"Bye, Alberto!", I said and he gave me a dazzling smile showing his teeth and I almost swoon.

We got up to leave and Everette seemed to have a permanent scowl plastered on his face.

He wrapped his hand tightly around my waist and dragged me out of the restaurant.

We both got inside the car and he still had scowl on his face and jaw was clenched and palm was folded into a fist and he was looking out of the window.

The silence inside the car was killing me so I finally asked, "Are you angry with me?"

He was still looking out of the window. "No."

"You are. What did I do?"

His jaw clenched even more and turned to me and inched his face closer.

"Would you like if I randomly go and flirt with a waiter?", he spat.

"Flirt? What do you mean?"

"Aeryn", he said in a firm tone. "You were flirting with that waiter while me, your husband was sitting right in front of you."

"I...I... wasn't flirting. I was just being friendly", I defended myself.

"I am not blind, Aeryn."

I chuckled nervously. "Why does it even bother you? And...I liked his smile, that's it. It is not a big deal."

His eyes furiously searched mine. "I am your husband, Aeryn."

"So?", I asked foolishly.

"Get this thing straight. You are married to me, you are bound to me and I won't tolerate you flirting with other men."

My mouth slightly parted. "You are jealous", I stated in a surprise tone.

He was taken aback by my words and he cleared his throat sitting back straight. "I am not."

I folded my arms. "Yes, you are."

"Shut up, Aeryn."

"Everette Wilbrose is jealous", I sang.

His head snapped to me and brought his face very close to mine, his breath tickled my lips. The tip of our noses brushed against each other.

"Shut your mouth, Aeryn or I'll shut it myself", he whispered; I could feel his words touching my lips.

And then he instantly pulled back.

His actions left me quite stunned to speak anything.

I silently sat there looking out of the window as the clouds rumbled and a lightning struck somewhere.

The road was empty, it was getting late at night when it started raining all of a sudden.

A smile formed on my face as the rain poured. I gently tapped the driver's shoulder. "Can you please stop the car?"

That caught Everette's attention. "What are you doing?"

"You will see."

Glaring at me he said to the driver, "Don't stop the car."

"Please!", I whined. "Please, stop the car."

The driver got nervous not knowing who to listen to.

I joined both my palms and literally begged him to stop the car and thankfully he parked the car at the side of the road.

Everette was giving me a deathly glare but ignoring him, I got out of the car.

The rain was pouring heavily and within seconds I was drenched from head to toe.

I stretched out my hands and threw my head back, feeling the rain drops on my face while slowly moving in circles.

I heard the car's door open and Everette stepped out with an umbrella.

"Aeryn, get inside the car", he ordered.

I grinned innocently. "No!"

He walked closer so that I was under the umbrella along with him.

I tried shoving him away but he didn't bulge.

"Just get inside, Aeryn", he said again and I frowned.

Exasperatedly I threw my hands up in the air and it hit the umbrella, the impact caused it to fall from his hand down on the road.

I giggled. "Oops."

He narrowed his eyes, the rain drenching him too. His hair became wet and rain drops fell down on his face making him look sexy despite the fact he was ready to kill me.

I took a step back and jumped around enjoying the rain and swirled around.

Everette was about to pick up the umbrella but I grabbed his hand, preventing him.

He yanked himself out of my hold. "I told you to not touch me."

My lips pressed into a thin line. "Why it is not a problem when you touch me but a problem when I touch you?"

"I have my reasons."

"Then you can shove your reasons up your ass", I retorted. "I will touch you, no matter what."

I took a few steps back and didn't let him affect my mood.

I again threw my head back and felt the rain drops on my face, lifting up my spirits promptly.

My mood changes very quickly and that's what happened because I went to Everette who was still standing in the rain, watching me carefully. His white shirt being wet, clung to his torso outlining his abs and and biceps.

I gulped and walked to him and held both of his palms in my hands.

"Come on, Everette", I urged. "Dance with me."

I then slowly intertwined my left hand with his right and placed my right hand over his shoulder.

He didn't make an effort to move. He was scrutinizing my face.

A minute passed by and we were still standing in that position; I felt rejected. Feeling embarrassed, I gulped and slowly detached myself from him but before I could do that, his left hand slipped around my waist and gradually his grip tightened and his right hand's fingers firmly intertwined with mine.

A small gasp escaped my lips as he pulled me closer, heat radiating from his body despite the rain pouring around us.

I bit my lips to stop my lips from curling up into a smile.

Our feets moved together at a leisurely pace, the sound of the rain drops hitting the road provided a music.

He slowly twirled me around and caught me back.

The intensity at which he was staring in my eyes scared me.

His grip around my waist tightened even more and he pulled me closer erasing the distance between us.

"How can you be so happy?", he whispered.

I opened my mouth to answer but nothing came out.

"Are you really happy with this marriage?", he asked in disbelief.

Our bodies and feets moved together in a rythmatic movement.

"I am not happy", I answered in a whisper. "I didn't want this marriage either."

"You always look happy; always jumping around", he stated.

"You don't always need a reason to be happy and besides...I have accepted this marriage. Like you said, I am bound to you now. I guess this is what destiny wanted and I can't do anything about it."

"And...", I added. "I married you mainly because of Carmel. I don't know what magic you casted on her, she likes you so much. She was delighted to know that I was marrying you. She needed a father, so, I married you."

His jaw clenched. "What if...what if someday we get a divorce?"

"If that's what destiny wants then I have no problem."

"You believe in destiny a lot." He leaned forward and rested his forehead against mine and closed his eyes. "Destiny is not always fair to us."

"That's what destiny is. It's not always fair but we can do nothing but accept it."

He sighed heavily and leaned backed. Our bodies came to a still, his hand slipped away from my waist and he took a step back.

"Can we go back now? Or you want to spend the night here?", he said sharply.

CHAPTER 8: Dad

A few days later...

Everette's POV:

Finally! I sighed in relief as the car stopped in front of my house.

After a week of getting my head eaten by my so called wife, I am finally home. At least she won't eat my head now.

The sound of her gasping made me realise that she was still with me. I rolled my eyes and stepped out of the car and she followed me, her jaw dropped on seeing the house.

"You live here?", she asked in surprise.

"No. That's just for show off. I live in a cottage."

"What?"

I rolled my eyes. "Obviously I live here. Don't ask stupid questions."

She grumbled underneath her breath before following me inside.

"Your house is amazing!", she exclaimed.

"I know", I said cockily.

"You could have said 'thank you' instead."

"What's the fun in that?"

She rolled her eyes and came closer. Standing in front of me, she slowly wrapped both of her hands around my neck and my breath hitched.

She inched her face closer. "You better stop being so cocky around me or you won't like the consequences."

"I don't like people with such attitude", she added.

"And I am not asking you to like me either", I said sharply.

She glared. "But unfortunately I have to live with you and I won't tolerate this attitude."

I smirked. "Don't forget you are in my house, not the other way around."

She opened her mouth to speak but was cut off by someone's clearing of throat. She instantly moved back and we turned towards the door where Gareth and Carmel stood.

"Sorry to disturb you guys but I was just dropping Carmel here", he said with a slight smirk on his face.

Carmel was bitting her lips to stop her from smiling.

"Thank you, Gareth", Aeryn said with a smile. "For dropping her."

"No problem, Aeryn." He then turned to Carmel and winked at her. "We are best friends now."

"Are you?", Aeryn asked Carmel and she nodded happily.

Carmel then came to Aeryn and they both hugged each other and Aeryn kissed her forehead and I couldn't help but smile seeing them.

I glanced at Gareth and he was already looking at me with a smirk on his face. My smile faded on looking at him and I gave him a glare.

The smirk turned into a grin and I rolled my eyes.

"Meet me in my study", I told him and walked upstairs to my study.

I sat down in my swivel chair and Gareth entered with his signature smirk on his face.

"Brother, brother, brother", he spoke dramatically. "It has been such a long time since I last saw you."

"It has been just a week, Gareth."

He ignored my statement. "You seem to be really happy. Did something happen in Australia?" He wiggled his eyebrows suggestively.

He took a seat opposite to me.

I massaged my temples. "Nothing that you think happened."

His lips curled downward. "Well, that's sad."

"Did you find her?", I asked hopefully.

"Finding someone whose name you don't even know is not easy."

"Did you find her? Yes or no?"

"Of course not! That's what I am saying."

Disappointment hit me hard. "Oh...any clue?"

He shook his head. "No, brother."

My palm folded into a fist. Why am I not able to find her?!

"It's not easy, brother. You should stop searching. It's impossible."

My head snapped to him. "If you don't want to help me search her, then don't. But stop discouraging me."

I sighed deeply. "I am just hoping that someday, I'll find her."

"You have been hoping for the past twenty years, Eve."

"And I can hope for another twenty years."

He leaned forward. "Hoping, sometimes, burn us. Slowly. Painfully."

A fire ignited in my eyes. "And I don't mind getting burnt by it."

"You are hurting yourself, Everette."

"I told you, I don't care!"

"Aeryn, she...she is good for you. Just accept her and forget about that girl."

"Aeryn is crazy. She acts like a teenager. In one week she ate up my head", I snapped. "I still have two and a half months, if I don't find her till then..."

"Then you are going to whole heartedly try and make this marriage work?", he completed for me.

I gulped. "Yes."

"But you are also going to give your full effort in finding her", I said.

"I am giving my full effort, brother. I even went to Austin, to that colony. I went to their house but they moved from there a long time back and no one knows where they went."

I held my face in my hands. "I need her, Gareth. I need her."

I heard him get up and he stood beside me and placed his hand on my shoulder in an assuring manner.

"What if she is already married?", he said.

I gritted my teeth and removed my face from my hands. I glared at him. "Are you consoling me or making me more sad?"

He lifted up his hand in surrender. "I was just stating a fact."

"I don't need your facts."

He walked away from me with his hands behind his back. "I can't believe you never asked her name!"

"I just forgot."

He turned to me. "Forgot? How can you not ask her name? If only you knew her name, everything would have been easier."

"I know...I know...", I said gloomily.

"I was thinking", he said. "Aeryn's eyes, they are brown too. She owns a restaurant...what if..."

I looked at him hopefully. "Is it possible?"

He shrugged his shoulders. "Maybe."

"Ask her to make you a cheese grilled sandwich", he suggested.

"She doesn't have that on her menu."

"It's a simple recipe, she must know it. Ask her to make it here."

"Or just ask her whether she once fed a boy a sandwich", he added.

"I am not telling her anything. I will just ask her to make the sandwich."

He hummed in response and made his way towards the door. "I am leaving. Will inform you if I get any clue."

"Okay", I whispered gloomily.

...

During night, after I showed Aeryn and Carmel their respective rooms, I knocked softly on Carmel's door.

"Come in!", came her reply.

I slowly opened the door and peeked in, she was sitting on the bed cross legged with a notebook in one hand and a pencil in the other.

I sat down beside her. "Am I disturbing you?"

He shook her head immediately and kept aside her notebook and pencil. "Of course not."

"This bed is so comfortable and the room is so beautiful; thank you so much, Eve", she expressed her gratitude.

I smiled. "Glad you liked it."

I eyed her notebook. "What are you making?"

She scratched her neck. "Some...umm...sketches."

"Can I see them?"

"Okay..." She picked up her notebook and flipping over to a page, she handed it to me.

My mouth parted in surprise looking at the sketch. She sketched me.

It was so perfect.

"That's awesome, Carmel! You are so good at it", I remarked.

She blushed. "Thanks!"

I handed the notebook back to her.

"Thank you, Eve for marrying mama", she said. "And...and for accepting me."

"You don't need to thank me for anything, okay? You are under my care now."

She nodded. And then she nervously started playing with her fingers.

"I...umm...wanted to ask something", she spoke nervously.

"What happened, Carmel?", I said in a worried tone.

She looked at me hopefully. "Can I call you...dad?"

For a second, my heartbeat stopped and then it started beating at a fast rate. My heart warmed and it skipped a beat.

A wide smile formed on my face. "Yes, yes you can."

She jumped on the bed happily. "Really?!"

"Yes!"

She jumped and hugged me tightly wrapping her arms around my neck. I hugged her back. "Thank you, dad."

My heart yet again skipped a beat when she called me dad. It feels so good.

Pulling back, she placed a kiss on my cheek.

Smiling, I got up to leave. I kissed her forehead lingeringly and muttered, "Goodnight, Carmel."

"Goodnight, dad."

Feeling satisfied, I left her room and came face to face with Aeryn. She was watching us.

I noticed some tears at the corner of her eyes.

I put my hands in my pocket and moved past her and she walked beside me quietly.

"Are you crying?", I asked and turned to her.

"No. I am just happy."

I raised a brow at her and she spoke, "Thank you."

"For what?"

Smiling through the tears, she stared at me. "For accepting Carmel as your daughter."

"Stop thanking me for that and get used to it."

She nodded and wiped away her tears. "Okay..."

Her hair was opened and I brushed a strand of stray hair behind her ear.

Before I could comprehend what I was doing, I leaned in and brushed my lips gently against her forehead.

"Goodnight", I whispered and quietly left.

CHAPTER 9: Cousin's Wedding

Aeryn's POV:

"So, you guys did nothing?"

I rolled my eyes. "No", I said much to Harper's disappointment.

"You didn't even kiss?"

"No!"

She frowned and her lips curled downwards. "That's so sad. I expected you to be pregnant by now."

While stirring the soup, I smacked her head. "Focus on the noodles!"

"Okay, okay."

"But...", she said after a pause. "Did you guys have some romantic moment atleast?"

My mind wandered off to the night we danced in the rain but I don't know whether to consider it romantic or not.

Harper's snapped her fingers in front of my eyes. "Lost in his thoughts again?"

I slapped away her hand. "No. Nothing happened nor do I want anything to happen."

She sighed. "You are still waiting for that boy, right?"

I smiled sadly and whispered, "I don't know..."

She placed her hand on my shoulder. "Look, Aeryn. I understand your feelings but...for how long will you wait for him? You are already married now, even if he decides to show up someday, you won't be able to do anything."

I blinked away my tears and sniffled. "What do you want me to do?"

"Just forget about him now. Remember it as a beautiful memory and cherish it. Okay?"

I nodded gloomily.

She gave me a small smile. "I know it will take you some time to forget him but when you do, focus on Everette. He is your husband now. Who knows you will start to like him slowly."

"He...umm...kissed my forehead last night saying goodnight", I told her.

"He did?", she asked excitedly.

"Yes."

She clapped her hands. "That's so cute!"

I bit my lips to stop myself from smiling at that thought.

"And? What else happened?"

"Last night, Carmel asked him whether she can call him dad or not and he said yes."

"He is so sweet!", she praised him.

"Something else also happened? Are you hiding something from me?", she urged and I finally told her everything that happened in Australia.

When I finished, Harper twirled around enthusiastically while smiling widely. "He is getting jealous already!"

"It won't be long before you guys kiss and have s--"

I slapped her shoulder as my cheeks turned red. "Shut up!"

...

It was 10:15 at night when I reached home. The house seemed quite and I was about to climb upstairs when I heard voices coming from the living room.

I walked to the living and the TV was on and a movie was going on, on the couch sat Everette and Carmel together with Everette's hand around Carmel's shoulder as they cuddled.

Their backs was towards me and I said softly, "Carmel?"

Everette turned to me immediately and placed his finger on his lips silencing me.

I quietly walked up to him to see that Carmel fell asleep while watching the movie.

He switched off the TV and slowly and carefully picked Carmel up in his arms and carried her upstairs with me following behind him.

Once inside her room, he placed her on the bed and covered her with the duvet and kissed her forehead before switching off the lights and leaving the room.

The silence was uncomfortable as he stared at me with his hands in his jeans pockets.

"Umm...did she have dinner?", I said referring to Carmel.

"She did", he replied.

"Oh...and you?"

He paused for a moment before saying, "I did."

"Good."

"You don't need to worry about her while you are at the restaurant. I will look after her when I am home and besides that, the housekeepers here are trustworthy, they also will look after her", he clarified.

I smiled softly. "Thank you."

"Stop thanking me, Aeryn."

"Sorry", I mumbled.

We stood silently for a minute and he ran his fingers through his hair before speaking.

"Can you make me a grilled cheese sandwich? Not right now though..."

I don't why he wants to eat that but I already know my answer.

"No. You can make it yourself. It's not difficult to make."

"I know... but can you make it?"

"No", I said coldly.

A few years back, I stopped making the cheese grilled sandwich because it always reminded me of him and I always used to end up crying.

"Fine", he muttered angrily.

I turned around to leave but he stopped me. "Listen."

"Yes?"

"My younger sister is getting married."

I raised a brow at him. "Younger sister? I thought you only had a brother."

"She is my cousin. I consider her and her elder brother like my real sister and brother."

"Oh, okay...so?"

"You need to come with me to Dallas for her wedding. You and Carmel."

"I can't go. I just came back from Australia and I can't leave my restaurant again", I argued.

"Your friend can take care of the restaurant."

"She is also a human. She already was taking care of it. She needs a break too."

He sighed. "It's important, Aeryn. You need to come with me or my mother will skin me alive."

"Take Carmel with you, if you want but I can't come with you."

He caught my wrist. "Try to understand. Please. You need to attend her wedding. They couldn't attend mine cause they were out of the country and the wedding was on a short notice but now they want to meet you."

I removed my wrist from his hold. "I can't leave my restaurant. That's final."

He pressed his lips in a thin line. "Fine. Then talk to my mother yourself. If she agrees then well and good."

"Okay", I agreed and he pulled out his phone and dialled his mother's number.

She picked up quickly and he told her that I was not ready to attend the wedding.

She said something to him and with a smirk on his face he handed the phone to me.

I gulped. "Hello?"

"Aeryn", she spoke sternly. "Why are you not attending the wedding?"

"Actually, Mrs Wilbrose, I need to--"

She cut me off. "Mrs Wilbrose?! You are calling me Mrs Wilbrose? Dare you call me that! You will call me mother. It's mother for you not Mrs Wilbrose! Understood?"

I stuttered, "Y-yes, Mrs...mother."

Everette stifled a laugh and his eyes shone with amusement.

"Better. Now, why are you not attending the wedding?"

"I need to look after my restuarant, mother. I can't leave it."

"Someone else can look after it for you. It's a matter of two days only."

"But--"

"I don't wanna hear any excuses. You are coming with Everette and Carmel day after tomorrow."

"B-but--"

"Bye, Aeryn. See you on Saturday!"

And the call ended; I looked at the phone in disbelief.

Everette took the phone from me with a grin on his face.

"I suppose you must need a dress for the wedding", he spoke.

I shoved his shoulder and walked away. "Shut up, jerk!"

He grabbed my arm and turned me around. He wrapped his arm around my waist making sure I don't run away.

He placed something in my palm and I saw his card.

"Buy a dress for the wedding", he said when I looked at his card in confusion.

I shoved the card back to his hand. "No, thanks. I can buy it myself."

"No. You will use my money for it not yours."

"Why? Are you afraid I don't have enough money to buy a decent dress and then I will turn up at the wedding in some weird dress and embarass you?"

His jaw dropped. "No! What are you talking about?"

I rolled my eyes. "I don't need your money."

Before he could say anything, I added, "And don't say that you bought my restaurant for me so indirectly I am using your money. That's different and I am going to return your money. Not at the moment but yes, in the future."

He sighed. "You don't need to pay me back."

"No, I am going--"

"Just forget I even bought the restaurant. Just forget. You don't need to return me the money. Okay?"

"But--"

He placed his index finger on my lips. "Shh..."

I gulped feeling his finger on my lips. His eyes fell on my lips and he slowly trailed down his finger from my lips, down to my chin and then slowly to my neck.

I sucked in a deep breath feeling his finger going down to the base of my neck and then thankfully, it abruptly stopped there.

Clearing his throat he pulled away his finger and handed me the card.

"Buy a--", he spoke but his voice sounded hoarse so he quickly cleared his throat again. "Buy a nice dress for you and Carmel, okay?"

He removed his hand from my waist and then again he leaned closer and kissed my forehead mumbling goodnight.

My heart skipped a beat and I somehow managed to whisper, "Goodnight."

He didn't hear it cause he was already walking away to his room.

CHAPTER 10: Discipline

* grins*

Everette's POV:

"Are we going in that?", Carmel questioned, her jaw dropped on seeing my private jet.

"Yes, Carmel. We are going in that."

I heard Aeryn mock, walking beside us. "Such a humble reply, Mr Wilbrose. Quite surprised you didn't say 'why not, afterall I am a billionaire'."

She was still pissed off about the fact that she was being taken there against her will although Carmel is very excited about it.

One side of my lips curled up. "I have saved those replies exclusively for you, Mrs Wilbrose."

She rolled her eyes. "Very funny." And walked past me making sure she bumped her shoulder against mine.

Carmel let out a chuckle. "She sometimes act like a kid."

"I know. It took everything in me to not murder her while in Australia."

Carmel gasped and bit her lips. "You really hate her?", she asked in a serious tone.

My eyes widened and I clarified. "No, no! I don't hate her...but she is very annoying. I was just kidding."

"Oh", she whispered but still she didn't look satisfied. She looked ahead and walked quietly.

"Carmel", I said softly and she turned her head to me. "I won't hurt her, ever. Don't worry about that. She is my wife and she is in my care now. Nothing will happen to her."

She gave me a toothy grin and side hugged me. "Thank you."

I leaned down and kissed her cheek. "The same goes for you. You are my daughter now. And I will always protect you both."

She gestured me to lean down and when I did, she kissed my cheek too.

Grinning she said, "I love you, dad."

And yet again my heart skipped a beat and it swelled with love.

I ruffled her hair and smiled. "I love you too, daughter."

"How can you guys forget me?!", came an annoying voice of my lovely brother.

I turned around to see him breathing heavily. "Don't you have your own jet to travel in, Gareth?"

"Oh, brother", he said placing his arm over my shoulder. "We should save energy, shouldn't we?"

"Or you wanted some alone time with your wife?", he whispered the last part, wiggling his eyebrows suggestively.

I elbowed him in his chest making him groan. "Fuck off, Gareth."

I grabbed Carmel's hand and dragged her with me. "Let's go."

"Okay, okay. Sorry", Gareth said running up to us.

I rolled my eyes. "Just don't eat my head during the flight."

He winked. "As you say, brother."

...

I slammed my head on the back of the seat in front of me.

Seems like Gareth forgot that he told me he won't eat up my head. Well, he is not actually eating my head but he, Aeryn and Carmel for the past twenty minutes have put the music on full volume inside the jet and are dancing their asses off.

Exasperatedly, I got up. "Okay, that's enough!", I bellowed.

They all froze in their places and Carmel paused the music.

"This is a plane not a club. Everyone sit down on their respective seats!"

Gareth and Carmel both pouted sadly but eventually sat down on their seats.

Aeryn being Aeryn kept standing their with her arms folded, her glare directed at me.

Ignoring whatever I said, she again resumed the music and started swaying her hips.

I took a deep breath to calm myself down.

This girl really tests my patience.

"Aeryn", I warned. "Stop the music and stop dancing."

Gareth and Carmel were sitting beside each other and now they both were looking at us curiously.

When she didn't listen, I went and stopped the music myself. Giving me a glare, she started it again.

I stopped it again and she started it again.

Aargh!

I had enough!

I bent down, grabbed her legs and threw her over my shoulder.

She shrieked and punched my back telling me to put her down. I didn't listen to her and walked us towards the bedroom at the back while Gareth and Carmel laughed at us.

I closed the bedroom's door and placed her on the bed and climbed on top of her, and pinned both her arms over her head.

She gasped and sucked in a sharp breath as her eyes widened.

The tip of our noses touched.

"You are really testing my patience, Aeryn", I spoke in a low voice.

Slowly and teasingly, I ran the tip of my nose down her jaw and down to her neck. She smelled amazing, like vanilla and honey. Running my nose down the crook of her neck, I nuzzled it there.

Lifting her T-shirt a bit, I placed my hand inside her T-shirt, on her waist and she gasped.

"Believe me, Aeryn", I said huskily. "If I start testing your patience, you will definitely not like it."

My fingers gently brushed her skin and I placed a light kiss on her neck. Her breath hitched and she shuddered.

My voice turned huskier. "It will leave you hot, sweaty and begging for more."

I couldn't stop myself from kissing her neck again. So, I did. I kissed the base of her neck. Involuntarily her head turned sideways giving me more access.

I peppered kisses along her neck although my mind was screaming, telling me to stop.

Just a minute more. I thought.

My lips moved upwards and under her ear, I lightly sucked her skin and then gently nipped it.

She moaned. I smirked.

Lastly, I gave a light tug to her earlobe with my teeth and pulled away.

I stood near the bed and watched her looking so vulnerable. Her eyes were tightly shut, she was sucking her lower lip between her teeth. Her fingers clutched the bedsheet firmly. Her face was flushed. And her chest was rising up and down as she breathed heavily.

It took her a moment to realise I have already pulled away.

When everything registered in her mind, she sprang up and sat on the bed looking at me in shock.

I winked. "I hope you learnt the lesson."

Her mouth fell apart and smirking to myself, I left the room.

Leaving the room, I realised that there are other people on the plane too.

I mentally face slammed myself. Gareth is going to tease me for the rest of my life.

Anyway, I went over to them, and tried not to give them attention. Walking past them I glanced towards them and they both were whispering to each other.

When they saw me, they stopped and Gareth glanced back towards the room and back at me.

I sat down a few seats ahead of them and picking up a magazine, used it to cover my face.

In a moment, Gareth was sitting beside me with a smirk on his face.

He took the magazine away from my hand and put it away.

And then he looked at his wrist watch. "You took just ten minutes. I thought you guys won't be finished untill we land."

Ignoring him, I picked up the magazine again but he snatched it away.

"Tell me, brother", he said. "Should I be expecting to see a baby bump on her soon?"

My jaw clenched. "The only thing you should be expecting is a punch on your nose."

"Brother, brother, brother", he spoke dramatically. "Why are you so serious all the time?"

"Brother, brother, brother", I said sarcastically. "Why are you so annoying all the time?"

He scowled making me smirk.

He opened his mouth to say something but Aeryn decided to show up. Gareth turned to look at her and she sat down quietly with Carmel.

Gareth was scrutinizing her face and said, "Hey, Aeryn. What happened under your ear?"

Her brows knitted together and she placed her hand under her ear and opening her phone, she checked it in the camera and her eyes widened when she realised I gave her a hickey.

Getting up instantly, she ran to the bathroom and Gareth burst into laughter.

"So, that's what you were doing", he said in between laughing.

I narrowed my eyes. "Stop it, Gareth."

He pulled both my cheeks. "Aww...my little brother is taking a interest in his wife."

"Firstly, I am elder than you. Secondly..." I reduced my volume making sure Carmel doesn't hear it. "I am not taking any interest in her. I was just discipling her. And thirdly, don't pull my cheeks!"

He again pulled my cheeks making me glare at him. "As you say, brother, as you say."

If he was not my brother, I would have murdered him a long time back.

He became silent and Aeryn came back. The hickey was no longer visible.

She marched up to me and said to Gareth, "Move away."

"Gladly." He got up and left and Aeryn sat in his place.

She jabbed a finger to my chest and whispered shouted so no one hears. "T-this won't happen again! I allowed it this time but there won't be a second time. Get this inside your head, Mr Wilbrose."

She fuming with anger and inched her face closer. "And if you think this will discipline me then you are wrong. It. Will. Not. I will continue to annoy you. Do what you can."

She stood up but I caught her wrist and pulled her down making her land on my lap.

I whispered in her ear. "Go on, annoy me but I don't think so Carmel will like to see what happened in the bedroom in front of her eyes. She is still young for that."

For a better reminder, I lightly grazed her ear with my teeth.

Gasping she got up and stomping her foot in anger and exasperation, walked back to her seat.

CHAPTER 11: You Are Mine

Aeryn's POV:

To my utter annoyance, Everette wrapped his arm around my waist the moment we stepped out of the car in front of the mansion.

I rolled my eyes mentally remembering we need to act like real couples here.

We moved towards the mansion and Carmel and Gareth followed behind us.

As we climbed the steps, the door was opened by Mrs Wilbrose or I should say mother and there were a few more people whom I didn't recognise.

"Oh, Aeryn!", mother exclaimed on seeing me. "I knew you would come."

As if you gave me another option.

It's not that I hate her but sometimes she sounds very scary.

I smiled and she engulfed me in a tight hug and pulling back she kissed my cheek.

Next she hugged Carmel and kissed her cheek too.

Mr Wilbrose, who actually doesn't speak much, came forward and greeted us.

Though I am not very familiar with all them but they all feel like family.

Next, I was introduced to Everette's uncle and aunt and their children, Elora and Zack.

Elora was beautiful. Red hair, green eyes, an innocent looking face. She looked perfect.

She gave me a friendly smile and side hugged me, saying thank you for coming here.

And then there was Zack, who looked like a younger version of Everette except the beard he had a clean shaved face (unfortunately, not as handsome as Everette) but completely like Gareth in his attitude.

He took my hand and kissed my knuckles and winked at me. Everette pulled me even more closer and his grip tightened around my waist.

Since I decided to ignore him all day, I didn't say anything.

"Eve", Zack said while staring at me. "Your wife is really beautiful. She looks more beautiful in person than in pictures."

I felt a blush creeping up my neck, not because of his words but because of the intensity with which he stared at me.

"Okay, everyone!", Everette's aunt spoke. "Everyone get freshened up quickly then we all can have dinner together. Zack, show them their rooms."

"Let's go", Zack said.

We all followed him upstairs to a long corridor with rooms on each side of it.

These guys are freaking rich!

Zack opened one of the rooms and gestured to us. "This is your room."

I wanted to argue, I don't want to share a room with this jerk but I gave Zack a fake, tight smile instead.

And he opened another room adjacent to it and turned to Carmel. "And this is for the little lady."

Carmel smiled. "Thanks, uncle."

"Oh, you are welcome, darling."

"By the way", he added. "Her room is connected to your room. There is a connecting door inside."

I nodded at him and he left telling us that dinner will be in twenty minutes.

I moved past Everette and went inside the room. The room was beautiful, there was a king sized bed in the middle with a small chandelier hanging at its top. The walls were painted in cream colour and there was a walk in closet and a bathroom.

Our luggages were already placed inside the closet. That was fast.

I picked out a pale pink colour, knee length dress with a boat neck, covered with sparkles and quickly changed into it. And opened my hair and applied a nude lipstick, and of course not forgetting to hide the fucking hickey that that jerk gave me.

Everette was still in the bathroom and leaving him behind I went to Carmel's room seeing whether she was ready or not.

Since she was ready, I took her hand in mine and we both walked downstairs.

Everyone was already seated on the dining table and were chatting among themselves, they paused on seeing us and I passed them a smile before taking a seat opposite to Zack and Carmel sat between me and Gareth.

The dinner was about to be served when Everette came dressed in a casual light blue t shirt and a pair of jeans.

Unfortunately the only seat available was the one beside me and he sat there.

There was silence as everyone ate quietly, the housekeepers served the dishes and they all were delicious.

"So, Aeryn", Zack said and I lifted my head to look at him. "Yes?"

"Wanna take a walk in the garden after the dinner?"

"I would love--"

"No, she won't", Everette cut me off and my grip on the spoon tightened.

I wanted to reply to him but I realised I was ignoring him. So I gave a sheepish smile to Zack and muttered, "Sorry."

He smiled. "No problem, Aeryn. We can go for a walk later." And winked.

"I swear, Aeryn if I met you before Eve did, I would have definitely married you", Zack flirted in front of everyone and my cheeks burnt.

"You are really--" He groaned all of a sudden and bending down rubbed his leg.

What happened?

From the corner of my eyes I saw Everette giving him a deathly glare. And they both glared at each other, refusing to back down but eventually, Zack lowered his gaze and continued eating.

Shaking my head lightly, I resumed eating.

...

I was the first one to finish eating and I politely left saying I was tired.

I went back to our room trying to ignore Everette as much as possible.

I was sitting at the edge of the bed when the door opened and he came in.

I instantly got up and moved towards the bathroom but as I was going to open the door, I was grabbed by my bicep and turned around and backed up against the door my so called husband who didn't look pleased.

He pressed himself to me so that my breasts were pressed up against his chest.

He slipped his one hand around my waist and the other was pressed on the door beside my head. "For how long will you ignore me?"

I decided not to answer him and removed my gaze from him and lowering my head focused on the floor.

The hand which was pressed against the door, lifted my chin up. "Look at me."

Even though he lifted up my chin, I refused to look at him.

"Aeryn", he said in a deep, intense voice causing the butterflies to erupt in my stomach.

How can someone's voice be so sexy?

The tone with which he called my name made me lift my eyes and make a contact with his.

I gulped realising our close proximity.

"Stop ignoring me", he spoke in a low, desperate voice.

Yet I refused to speak.

When I didn't speak he said, "See, that's what I am talking about. You are not replying to me. You are not talking to me. What happened to the Aeryn I married who had to give a reply to my every sentence?"

It irritated me completely. "If I speak, it's a problem. If I don't speak, then it's a problem. What do you want me to do?"

He smiled. He literally smiled. A mischievous one. "It worked. You spoke."

I tried shoving him away but instead he pressed himself even more to me making me gasp.

He pushed my hair away to one shoulder and brushed his finger under my ear where he earlier gave me a hickey. "Why did you hide it?"

"I didn't want everyone to see it."

His gaze locked with me again. "You should have left it like that."

"Why?", I whispered.

"So they know you are mine", he said huskily.

"I am not yours."

"You are, Aeryn. You are my wife. I don't like it when someone tries to flirt with you. I should be the only one to compliment about your beauty."

Did he just call me beautiful? My heart fluttered.

"You never complimented me", I complained.

He nuzzled his nose in the crook of my neck and whispered hoarsely against my neck. "You are looking fucking beautiful right now, Aeryn. You always do."

I bit my lips to stop myself from smiling like a fool, and I blushed.

"Thanks."

I felt him smile against my neck before he started sucking there. It sent an electric jolt through my body and my fingers automatically found their way to his hair.

He kissed, sucked and nipped the base of my neck making me moan.

I was too lost in that feeling to realise it's wrong.

"Everette", I wanted to say it as a protest but it came out like a moan and I mentally cringed.

I placed my hand on his shoulder and tired pushing him away. "P-please..."

He stopped and lifted his head. "Please what? You want more?"

I breathed. "No."

"That's sad but no problem, wifey."

He then brushed his finger over the hickey he just gave me and he smirked. "Dare you hide it. I want everyone to see it."

"And", he added. "Stay away from Zack."

"He is your cousin."

He sighed. "I know but he is flirting with you a lot. I don't like it. Just don't talk to him much."

"What's the use of all this, Everette?"

"Huh?"

I gulped before saying. "In the end, you will divorce me. Why does it bother you whether someone is flirting with me or not? Whether everyone knows I am yours or not? In the end, I will be nothing to you."

His mouth slightly parted in surprise and his eyes narrowed. An unreadable emotion flashed across his face and for a moment, he looked zoned out.

His jaw clenched and palm folded into a fist. He pushed himself away from me and without giving me another glance, he left the room slamming the door shut.

CHAPTER 12: Confused

Everette's POV:

Everyone seemed to be asleep. The mansion was quiet. I walked out and went to the garden.

I kicked at the ground feeling disgusted with myself. I ran my hand down my face.

What am I doing?

She is right. In the end, I will divorce her and I literally told her: you are mine.

She might be my wife but she is not mine.

But...I feel jealous everytime I see someone flirting with her.

It's just because she is my wife. I assured myself.

Lost in my thoughts, I sat down on the grass thinking about how I am feeling like a mess right now.

Feeling tired, I layed down on the grass on my back and stared at the sky, at the full moon which was shining brightly.

A sigh escaped my lips as I put both my hands under my head.

Minutes passed by and I heard someone's footsteps. I didn't even bother to turn and look.

It stopped near my head and I looked up to see Gareth standing there with a poker face with his hands in his sweatpant's pockets.

Ignoring him, I stared at the sky again.

Without saying anything, he layed down beside me on his back and copying me, he put both his hands under his head.

"Brother", he said sarcastically. "You look upset."

"I am not in a mood to tolerate you, Gareth", I said coldly.

He looked taken aback by the coldness in my voice.

His elbow nudged mine. "What's wrong?"

"Don't know...", I whispered sadly. "I'm confused."

"Is it about Aeryn?"

I rolled my eyes. "Of course. Who else?"

"Oh..."

"Gareth?"

"Yes, brother?"

"Did you find any clue about her?"

He shook his head. "No, brother."

Yet again, I felt the disappointment running through my veins but somewhere there was this voice which seemed to be celebrating. Celebrating that I still have no clue about her, that the time is getting over and soon, I'll be bound to Aeryn forever.

Gareth propped himself up by the support of his elbow and stared at me. "Brother...what happened to you? I am trying to find her... don't be disappointed."

"It's not about her."

"Then?"

"I'm confused", I reitarated.

His tone became impatient. "About what, Everette?"

"About Aeryn and this girl."

"Are you in love with Aeryn?"

"No!", I spat. "But...but..."

"But you started to feel something for Aeryn, right?"

"No...but I told her she is mine and she said it's of no use because in the end, I will be divorcing her."

His face puzzled. "I don't understand."

"You said if we find that girl within three months, I can divorce Aeryn and marry her. And if I don't then I am going to accept Aeryn as my wife whole heartedly."

"So?"

"What if we find that girl within the next two months and then I will be divorcing Aeryn..."

"I still don't understand."

I sighed heavily. "What if...I don't want to divorce Aeryn? Then what? And what about Carmel? She is my daughter, I love her. I can't leave her."

A small smile formed on his face. "You are falling for her, brother."

"It's not about falling for her, Gareth. It's about getting attached."

I added. "And on the other hand, I am dying to meet that girl again, I want to marry her...but then there is Aeryn. Thinking about all those times I touched Aeryn intimately, I feel like I am betraying that girl."

"You are thinking too hard, brother. You are not betraying her. She was in the past, you can't spend your whole life waiting for her."

"I love her, Gareth."

"Aeryn?"

I glared. "That girl. My brownie."

"It's okay to feel love for her. But that was years back... twenty years back. Live in the present now."

He then stood up. "I will still continue to look for her. If I don't find her, then... it's Aeryn for you forever. But if I do find her, then..." He trailed off.

"Then what?"

He shrugged his shoulders. "I also don't know."

I stared at him blankly and he let out a small chuckle. He then extended his arm for me to take and placing my hand in his, I got up.

"We still have two months. Don't think so hard, you will get sick. If we find that girl we will see what we have to do about it."

"And... about Aeryn", he said. He patted my chest. "Let your heart guide you. Don't let the mind interfere."

"Let the heart guide where?", a voice said behind us.

We both turned back and saw Zack standing there. Seeing him reminded me of earlier this night when he was flirting with Aeryn and I scowled, my jaw clenched.

My blood boiled. In a few strides I was in front of him and I grabbed his collar almost lifting him off the ground. His eyes widened as he struggled to get out of my hold.

"If I see you flirting with my wife ever again, I will forget you are my brother and won't hesitate to kill you in front of everybody", I threatened through gritted teeth.

"It's not my fault! Gareth told me your marriage was arranged. He asked me to flirt with Aeryn to make you jealous", he confessed in a hurry.

I left his collar making him stumble backwards.

Behind me Gareth hissed. "Zack, you traitor!"

Furiously I turned to him and growled. "Gareth!"

"Sorry, brother!", he shouted before he started running and I chased him.

I chased him around the garden and while running he stumbled upon a rock but didn't fall instead his spectacles fell off and broke.

His steps faltered and I took the opportunity to jump on him making us both fall on the ground with me above him.

I punched his jaw, not too hard. "I hate you!"

He rubbed his jaw. "I love you too, brother."

Behind us Zack laughed and I gave him a glare making him cough as he masked his laughter.

I got off Gareth and went over to him and he panicked. "What did I do now?!"

I punched him in the jaw too and he groaned.

"I am going to complain this to aunty", he said.

Gareth exclaimed, "Me too! He broke my spectacles."

"No one is complaining this to anyone!"

"Zack, run!", Gareth shouted getting up and they both ran back inside.

I chased them trying to stop them from telling this to mother.

But luck wasn't on my side because mother whom I assumed was asleep was standing in the kitchen pouring herself a glass of water.

Both of them ran to her and hid behind her.

"What's going on here?", she questioned.

"Gareth. Zack", I warned.

Zack made the most innocent face and showed her his jaw where I punched him and a little bruise was forming there. "See, aunty. He punched me."

"And he broke my spectacles and punched me too", Gareth complained showing her his broken spectacles.

"I didn't break your spectacles!"

"But indirectly it is your fault!"

"Everette!", mom's voice silenced me.

"Yes, mother?", I said softly.

She placed both her hands on her waist. "Why are you punching them, huh? They are your brothers. You are married now, you even have a daughter but you still haven't grown up!"

"They are assholes!"

She gasped. "Everette!"

And I flinched and the both of them snickered.

"Apologise to them", she ordered. "And buy Gareth a new spectacles."

"First ask them what they did. That son of yours asked Zack to flirt with Aeryn to make me jealous."

"So? Did it make you jealous?"

"Mother", I said in disbelief.

She raised her brow. "Did it make you jealous?"

I gritted my teeth. "Yes."

"So, what's the problem in that? At least it made you realise how much you love her."

My mouth fell open. My eyes shone with surprise. "Mother…"

She walked to me and placed her hand on my shoulder and said in a low voice. "I know your marriage was an arranged one."

You gotta be kidding me! That Gareth even told her. I looked over her shoulder and gave Gareth a deathly glare.

"No", mother said. "He didn't tell me. I figured it myself."

My jaw dropped. "How?"

She patted my cheek with a small smile on her face. "I just know. You guys are really bad at acting as real couples. Anyone can make out."

"Who else knows?"

"Just me. Don't worry your secret is safe with me."

I sighed in relief. "Thanks, mother."

She gestured towards them. "Now, apologise to them."

I scoffed. "I am going to sleep."

Before she could hold me back and order me to apologise to them, I ran from there.

As I closed the door of my room mother's words rang in my ear. At least you realised how much you love her.

I scoffed to myself. I don't love her.

I shut out all those thoughts for the night and went inside the bathroom taking a glance at Aeryn who was fast asleep on the bed.

Changing into a pair of sweatpants and leaving my upper half naked, I walked out and slipped in the bed beside her.

Before laying down, I took a moment to look at her. She was lightly snoring, her mouth parted, chest slowly moving up and down. Her pink, luscious lips which made me wanna kiss her.

I leaned down and kissed her forehead lingeringly but it didn't satisfy me so I kissed both her cheeks and her nose scrunched up and brows knitted together as she snuggled closer to me.

A small chuckle left my mouth and I gently stroked her hair before laying down facing her.

Unconsciously, she buried her head in my chest and I wrapped my arm around her waist pulling her closer.

"Why are you making my heart go wild?", I barely whispered in her ear and placing one last kiss on her forehead, I let the sleep consume me.

...

"What the hell?!", someone screamed in my ear.

Then I was being hit on my arm ruining my peaceful sleep. "Leave me, jerk!"

I opened my eyes and saw Aeryn's panicked face which was inches apart from me.

"What?", I said hoarsely and she glared making me realise I had one of my arm around her waist and one of my leg was wrapped around her hips pulling her extremely closed to me.

Instead of pulling back, I gave her a smile placing a kiss on her jaw. "Good morning, wifey."

Her whole body stiffened. "L-leave me."

I lightly smirked. "What if I don't?"

"I'll bite you then!"

My mind being in the gutter imagined her over me while she bites my neck giving me hickeys.

My smirk widened. "If you are talking about giving me hickeys then go ahead. I won't mind it."

Her jaw dropped and she started hitting my arm; I flipped her over and climbed on top of her burying my face in the crook of her neck.

"If you are not going to bite me then I'll bite you", I whispered.

Saying that I nipped her neck and she half-moaned. "Eve-rette...no!"

Much to Aeryn's relief I was interrupted by a knock on the door.

She used all her might and pushed me away before getting up. "Y-yes?"

The door opened cautiously and Carmel's head popped in. "Um...grand ma asked me to call you both down for breakfast."

Aeryn got up hurriedly. "Yeah...we are coming."

"Okay", Carmel said before going away.

Giving me a glare, Aeryn stomped off to the bathroom.

...

Since it was the wedding day, more guests started to gather in the mansion but we all had a private family breakfast together.

Aeryn went down before me and when I walked into the dining area I spotted Gareth with a new pair of spectacles on his face and Zack standing together talking.

Walking past them I muttered, "Sorry."

Without glancing at them I walked to the table when Gareth shouted, "We already forgave you, brother!"

I rolled my eyes but eventually a smile formed on my face. Unfortunately, I love them.

I took a seat beside Aeryn as I was going to start eating, I heard a voice of an even more annoying person than Gareth.

"Eve!"

CHAPTER 13: Jealousy

Aeryn's POV:

An annoying femenine voice reached our ear. "Eve!"

Everyone turned to the dining room's entrance, there stood a tall, blonde hair woman. Long legs, perfect figure, she looked like a model wearing a tight champagne colour dress that hugged her figure like second skin reaching till her thigh.

She had a wide smile plastered on her face and her attention only on Everette.

"Oh, Everette", she dramatically while walking towards him. "I missed you! It has been such a long time since we met."

I watched with wide eyes as she wrapped her arms around Everette's neck hugging him tightly.

And then she kissed his cheek.

My lips pressed into a thin line.

Who the fuck she is?!

How dare she kissed him while I, his wife is sitting right beside him.

Everyone was looking at them and to be honest they both looked good together, like they are made for each other.

My heart clenched. I felt self-conscious.

When she pulled away, she still had her hand on his shoulder in an intimate manner.

"I'll see you after the breakfast", she said in a saccharine tone and then...she pecked his lips before walking away from the dining room.

Everette's body froze. My jaw dropped so did everyone else's.

Everette had a poker face on, Gareth and Zack looked at me worriedly.

It doesn't effect me. It doesn't effect me. I kept chanting in my mind. I closed my eyes taking deep breaths to calm myself.

Hell it effects me!

I dropped the fork and the knife on my plate and pushing back the chair, I got up.

Before anyone could stop me, I was walking back to our room.

Tears welled up in my eyes. She kissed him. He never kissed my lips but she, whoever the fuck she was, kissed his lips and he said nothing.

It's not I am dying to kiss him but...I am his wife. She can't do that.

Instead of going to our room, I went inside Carmel's and sat down on the edge of the bed.

I wiped away the tears with the back of my palm. I won't cry for that jerk.

Minutes later, there was a knock on the door.

"Go away, jerk!", I shouted.

The door opened slowly. "Mama?"

My tone softened. "Carmel?"

She came inside, a gloomy look on her face and she sat beside me.

She scrutinized my face. "You were crying?"

"No, Carmel. I would never cry for that jerk."

"It's not his mistake, mama", she defended him.

"Seriously? You now love him more than me?"

"I love you both equally but it's that girl's mistake. She kissed him. Eww."

I slowly nodded. "Yeah...eww..."

She chuckled making me chuckle too.

"How can she kiss him?!", I muttered to myself angrily.

"You are jealous", Carmel remarked.

"I am not!", I snapped.

She smiled mischievously. "You like him."

"No!"

She got up and twirled around happily. "You like dad", she drawled and my cheeks burnt red. "I don't!"

"Then why are you jealous?"

"I didn't say I am jealous."

"Then why are you so bothered if she kissed him?" She wiggled her eyebrows.

"Because he is my husband."

Someone knocked. "Aeryn?"

"Tell him to go away", I said to Carmel and she nodded before opening the door and without saying anything to him, she left leaving me alone with Everette.

Traitor!

Everette had a plate in his hand and coming inside he closed the door behind him and set the plate on the nightstand adjacent to the bed.

Huffing angrily, I folded my arms and turned my head sideways so that I don't see his face.

Instead of sitting beside me, he kneeled down in front of me. And took both of my palms in his hands. I tried yanking it out of his grip but he held them tightly.

"Aeryn", he said softly. "Look at me."

When I didn't turn my head he said in a sincere tone. "I am sorry, Aeryn."

My head snapped to him. "What?"

"Sorry. She kissed me all of a sudden, I didn't have the time to react."

"Who's she?", I questioned coldly. "Your girlfriend?"

"I am married to you. How can she be my girlfriend?"

"Who knows?"

"She is not my girlfriend", he stated.

"Then? Ex-girlfriend?"

"No."

I was losing my patience. "Then who is she?!"

"She is uncle's friend's daughter, Kathryn."

I gritted my teeth. "I am asking what relation she has with you."

He sighed. "I was drunk. I slept with her. End of the story."

My nose scrunched up in disgust. "You like her, huh?"

He scoffed. "No. She has been trying to cling to me ever since. I don't like her."

I rolled my eyes. "You know what, you should have married her only. You both look good together."

He cupped my cheek and gently caressed it with his thumb and stared intensely in my eyes. "I would rather tolerate you for the rest of my life than marrying her."

My cheeks slightly warmed up. "Is that a compliment?"

A small smile touched his lips. "Maybe."

I slapped his hand away. "It's not about tolerating. You must find her beautiful, don't you? After all she has a model like figure."

"Is it jealousy in your tone, wifey?"

"Not a chance."

He got up and sat beside me. "Aeryn...you don't have to feel self-conscious about yourself. You are my wife, no other woman can catch my attention other than you. You are beautiful in your own way."

He brushed away a strand of hair from my face. "And I don't care about how you look because you are one of the kindest person I ever met. Your heart shines, it makes you sparkle. It makes you unique."

My face was as red as a tomato, my eyes welled up with tears. His words touched my heart and soul.

Yet I said, "Stop buttering me!"

He sighed shaking his head. "It took me a lot of time to mug up those lines from Google and not even a single thank you."

I smacked his arm in frustration. "Jerk! Go away!"

And here I was thinking he said all those things from his heart.

I continued smacking him and he started laughing. "Sorry, sorry! I was just kidding! I didn't mug up those lines from Google!"

"I don't believe you!"

"I swear, Aeryn. I said it from my heart. I was just messing with you."

I stopped smacking him and huffed.

He picked up the plate and cut a piece of the omelette and extended the fork towards my mouth. "You didn't even have breakfast."

I puffed up my cheeks. "I am not hungry."

He didn't listen to me and brought the fork to my lips. "Please?", he requested sweetly.

Giving him a glare I opened my mouth and ate it making him smile.

He cut another piece and fed me and my heart fluttered at his actions.

The boyish grin on his face made him look younger and my heart beated wildly in my chest.

...

Everette asked me whether I need any makeup artist or someone to help me dress up but I refused.

But now standing infront of the mirror, I feel nervous. The dress is beautiful but thinking about Kathryn and how beautiful she is I feel anxious about how I am looking.

Whether I like to accept it or not, I want Everette to notice me. I want him to find me beautiful. I want him to find me attractive. Just him. Only him. Because he matters alone to me.

I styled my hair in a rough bun and wore a small diamond pendant when there was a knock at the door.

He is here.

Taking in a deep breath, I opened the door and my breath hitched on seeing him dressed in a black tuxedo looking handsome as always.

He took his own sweet time in running his eyes all over my body sensually making it linger on my legs visible due to the slit.

He stepped forward and taking my hand he pulled me back inside the room.

He grabbed my waist, pulling me closer and rested his head on my shoulder. He placed a small kiss there and continued showering kisses all over my neck making my knees weak.

"Damn it, Aeryn", he whispered huskily against the base of my neck. "You are looking stunning."

I felt happy knowing he approved of how I am looking.

"Am I?", I whispered.

He removed his head from my neck and cupped both my cheeks and kissed my forehead. "Yes."

I smiled. "You would be glad to know you are looking good too."

He smirked. "Oh, really? I didn't know it."

I scowled shoving him but he wrapped his arm around my waist possessively.

"Let's go", he said as we walked out of our room.

"Where's Carmel?", I inquired.

"She already went with Gareth."

"Oh."

The wedding ceremony was at night in the garden only and it was beautifully decorated with white and pink roses.

"By the way", Everette said. "Mother already knows about our marriage. She found out."

I gasped. "Are we in trouble?"

He looked at me. "Thankfully, no. But she says we are terrible at acting like real couples."

I folded my arms. "Are you blaming me?"

"You literally kept ignoring me in front of everybody when we arrived here", he accused.

"Can you blame me? It was your mistake. You deserved it."

By now we both were glaring at each other when all of a sudden Gareth came and wrapped his one arm around Everette's shoulder while the other around mine.

He acted as if he was normally talking to us while giving a fake smile to everyone who walked past us.

"Stop arguing for God's sake!", he whispered shouted. "Everyone will start suspecting."

"He started it", I said pointing towards Everette.

Everette hissed. "It was your mistake!"

"Oh my goodness! Shut up!", Gareth interrupted. "Both of you are looking as if you can't wait to kill each other. Smile!"

Still glaring at Everette, I smiled tightly. And he did the same thing.

"Stop glaring!", Gareth scolded.

I took a deep breath and softened my features but Everette refused to stop giving me a glare.

When Gareth realised that Everette won't calm down easily, he pointed to a random direction. "Oh, look, Eve! Mr Grapes is there. Let's meet him."

Gareth grabbed his bicep firmly and started dragging him and Everette yanked himself out of his grip and scowled. "I don't know any Mr Grapes."

Gareth didn't give up and grabbed his bicep even more firmly and finally dragged him away. "Oh, come on...you will get to know him. Nice, tangy, juicy-juicy Mr Grapes."

I rolled my eyes at him and saw Carmel walking towards me in her dark red, plain gown.

"I thought you guys already resolved your fight", she said.

I huffed. "We did but that jerk blamed me saying because of me his mother now knows that are marriage was arranged."

"Grandma knows?", she asked in a surprised tone.

"Yes."

"Oh..."

We heard the music playing and we all focused our attention to Elora and her father who had their arms hooked and walked down the aisle.

She glanced at Carmel and me and smiled softly and we mirrored her smile.

Her dad handed her hand over to her fiance and the ceremony started.

It went on and finally the priest said. "I now pronounce you husband and wife. You may now kiss the bride."

Elora's fiance firstly stared into her eyes before capturing her lips and we all clapped and cheered.

Time passed by and I didn't get to face Everette again, thankfully!

There was a good number of guests and I couldn't locate Everette, not that I was looking for him.

The bride and the groom were having their first dance and we all gathered around to watch them.

Later when they were finished and other couples joined the dance floor, I turned to leave but something caught my attention.

Everette and Kathryn.

Their fingers were intertwined and Kathryn pulled him with her to the dance floor.

I watched as Everette wrapped his arm around her waist pulling her closer making my blood boil.

They both were waltzing to the music and Everette didn't look irritated instead his lips were curled up in a smile while they both stared into each other's eyes.

I am not going to stand here and watch them and do nothing.

I roamed my eyes around the garden and located Zack having a drink at the bar.

I went over to him. "Zack?"

He put down the glass on the counter. "Yes, Aeryn?"

I smiled. "Can you dance with me?"

His eyes widened. "I did drink a bit but I am not drunk enough to dance with you and get myself killed by your husband."

I fought the urge to roll my eyes. "Come on! He won't do anything. Besides he seem to be rather busy himself." I spat the last sentence and his eyes went over to the dance floor where they both were still dancing.

"Oh...", he muttered when he realised what I mean to do. "I understand."

He stepped closer and held my hand. "Let the fun begin."

We both walked over to the dance floor and he wrapped his arm around my waist and I placed my hand over his shoulder and to make it look more intimate I moved my hand upward and lightly wrapped it around his neck.

I was facing them as we both waltz.

At first he didn't notice but then when his gaze fell on us, his eyes narrowed.

He stopped paying attention to whatever Kathryn was saying and kept staring us and I pretended to chuckle at something Zack said.

"Did he see us?", Zack whispered.

"Yes."

Zack twirled me around and caught me back and Everette scowled.

His jaw was clenched and when Kathryn tried seeking his attention he mumbled something to her and started walking towards us.

"He is coming", I told Zack in a whisper.

His face showed fear. "If I die today, tell everyone I died doing a noble cause."

His words this time genuinely made me chuckle. "Okay."

His steps faltered when Everette placed his hand on his shoulder firmly.

Dropping my hand, Zack turned to him.

"Zack", Everette said with a fake smile and a warning in his eyes.

Zack gulped and whispered, "All yours, brother." That was it before he ran for his life.

Everette didn't say anything to me and his hands slipped around my waist roughly pulling me closer to him and I crashed with his chest.

When I looked at him, he was glaring down at me.

He started swaying us slowly, intertwining our fingers, pretending to dance like couples. Real couples.

He still didn't say anything and kept dancing making me forcefully dance too.

And then finally he hissed. "Done flirting with Zack?"

"Done flirting with Kathryn?", I retorted.

If looks could kill, I would have been dead by now. His eyes were burning with anger.

Much to his frustration, I gave him a saccharine smile. His grip firmed on my waist.

He leaned closer and growled in my ear as a warning. "Aeryn!"

I battered my eyelashes. "Yes, Everette?"

His lips pressed into a thin line as his eyes continued to shoot daggers.

All of a sudden, Gareth jumped on the dance floor and ran over to us and again wrapped one of his hand over Everette's should and the other over mine.

"Brother, brother, brother", he spoke while pretending to laugh at something we said. Then he gritted his teeth. "What are you both doing?"

"Someone's a little jealous, that's it", I taunted.

Everette opened his mouth to speak but Gareth quickly cut him off. "Brother! Did you meet Mr...um...Mr Banana over there. Come on, I will introduce you. You will love him, sweet and creamy."

He grabbed both his shoulders and forcefully dragged him away to a random direction.

As I got away from the dance floor, mother grabbed my arm and dragged me to quiet corner. "What's going on between you two?"

I fidgeted with my fingers. "Umm...just a little fight..."

"Little? You both are creating drama. Everyone has started to question us."

I felt guilty and lowered my head. "Sorry, mother."

She gently placed her palm over my cheek. "Look, Aeryn. I know this marriage was arranged. I knew it from the beginning. Everette never dated anyone and it worried me. He never used to take interest in a woman or get jealous over her. But ever since you married him, he changed. He is possessive about you. He smiles secretly while looking at you. You changed him."

She continued, "I want you both to make this marriage work. I don't want my son to lose a gem like you. And I am sure he loves you but he is just afraid to accept it."

He loves me?

As she finished, I was left speechless.

She patted my cheek. "Just try, okay?"

I nodded. "I'll try, mother."

She was about to leave when she said, "Oh, and one more thing. Don't forgive him easily." And then she winked making me chuckle.

CHAPTER 14: Asshole

Aeryn's POV:

She was about to leave when she said, "Oh, and one more thing. Don't forgive him easily." And then she winked making me chuckle.

Feeling a little better, I walked back to the main crowd and by now I couldn't spot anyone familiar.

A waiter passed by me with a tray having red wine, I took a glass from him and drank it in one go.

I took another glass of red wine from another waiter. And in one corner, I spotted Everette along with Kathryn who was clinging onto his arm.

My grip tightened on the glass and in anger I gulped it down quickly.

I replaced the empty glass with another glass of red wine, my eyes shooting dagger at both of them as Kathryn seductively ran her fingers up and down his arm.

Before I knew it, I already had four glasses of wine. I should have thought about that before cause I am lightweight.

I took a step towards them and my feet wobbled. I closed my eyes and tried to prevent myself from falling.

Thinking I was okay now, I took another step towards them and my knees buckled. I was about to fall but Carmel was quick to hold my hand and prevent me from falling.

"Mama, are you okay?"

My whole attention was on them, my eyes welled up with tears. Carmel followed my gaze and looked at them.

"Oh", she whispered.

A tear fell down my cheek. "I hate him!"

"Mama, don't cry, please..."

"No woman can catch my attention other than you", I said bitterly. "That's what he told me."

I couldn't stop the tears from falling and Carmel said, "Can you walk back to your room?"

I tried walking and my knees buckled again, if not for Carmel, I would have definitely fallen down this time.

"You wait here, I will call someone."

"Anyone but him", I gritted looking at him.

"Okay...just stay here..." Saying that she ran somewhere and I stayed there, tears falling from my eyes watching them both together.

They both were talking, and Everette was laughing at something she said.

A minute passed by and I saw Gareth and Carmel running to me.

Gareth wrapped his arm around my shoulder. "Let's get you to your room."

He helped me walk back to my room and Carmel walked beside us looking worried.

Once inside the room, he made me sit on the edge of the bed and I buried my face on his shoulder and burst into tears.

He slowly rubbed circles on my back trying to soothe me.

"Am I not worth him?", I cried.

"No, Aeryn", he said softly. "He is not worth you."

"He told me he doesn't like her yet he was talking with her", I sobbed.

"I feel jealous", I said. "She is so beautiful and then there is me. He would never give me that attention."

Third Person's POV:

Never in his life Gareth felt so much anger for his brother. Seeing Aeryn crying kept fueling it.

Their mother always taught them to never ever disrespect a woman. And he made her cry, that too she is his wife. Not some random woman.

"Aeryn, there is no comparison between you and Kathryn. She might be beautiful but she doesn't have a heart as beautiful as yours. And believe me when I saw you today in this gown, I swear I drooled but then I realised you are already married...well... that's a different story."

Aeryn chuckled softly through her tears and Gareth placed a small kiss on the top of her head and got up.

"Look after her", he told Carmel.

"Where are you going?", Aeryn questioned.

He removed his coat and placed it on the chair in the corner of the room and rolled up the sleeves of his shirt. "To deal with someone."

He left her room and walked downstairs. The lobby was empty since everyone was outside and he saw Everette walking towards him from the other end.

They both stopped in front of each other.

"Have you seen Aeryn?" Everette's question made him even more angrier.

In a moment, Gareth's fist connected with Everette's jaw, the impact causing him to stumble a few steps back.

When he recovered from the shock, he growled. "What the fuck, Gareth?!"

He marched to Gareth and gripped his collar. "Why the fuck did you punch me?!"

"For being an asshole", he replied clearly not effected by how firmly Everette held him by his collar.

He removed his hand from his collar. "I didn't do anything!"

Gareth folded his hands. "Really? Care to tell what you were doing with Kathryn?"

"That was nothing."

"Nothing? But it seemed you suddenly started liking her", he mocked.

"I don't like her! It was just to make Aeryn jealous. I wanted to irritate her."

Gareth stepped closer and patted his chest a little too harshly with a tight, fake smile on his face. "Congratulations, brother. Your plan worked; you made your wife cry."

Everette's face puzzled. "Cry?"

"Yes, cry. I hope you have to beg for her forgiveness", he cursed and turning around, left leaving Everette who felt the guilt consuming him.

...

Aeryn's POV:

After changing my clothes to a t-shirt and shorts, I layed down on the bed keeping my head on Carmel's chest and wrapping my arm around her shoulder.

"Mama?"

"Hmm?"

"Are you sure you don't have any feelings for him?"

"I hate him, Carmel. Is that enough for a feeling?"

"No...I mean...I think you like him. That's why you were so jealous--"

"Carmel, shut your mouth", I scolded.

"Okay...sorry...", she whispered.

A knock on the door sounded through the room. Thinking it to be Gareth I said, "Come in."

The door opened cautiously and Everette's head popped in and my jaw clenched. Carmel and I got up and sat up straight.

He nervously scratched the back of his neck while walking further into the room.

Carmel got down the bed and moved past him.

"Carmel?", he said in surprise.

She folded her arms angrily. "I am angry with you, dad."

"You also?"

She nodded. "Unless and untill mama doesn't forgive you, I won't talk to you."

She moved to the door and Everette called her,"Carmel, listen."

"Goodnight, dad", she said without even looking at him and left the room.

He sighed and came and sat a little too close to me on the bed. Trying to creat some distance between us, I crawled back on the bed and he moved forward.

This continued untill my back hit the headboard of the bed and he placed both his hands on either side of my head caging me.

None of us spoke and he just continued to stare into my eyes and then lifting his hand, gently brushed away a drop of tear which remained in the corner of my eyes with his thumb.

"I didn't want to make you cry", he whispered, guilt lacing his tone.

"But I did."

"I know and I am..."

"Sorry?"

He nodded slowly. "Yes. I am sorry, Aeryn."

"You apologised this morning for the same thing yet you repeated it."

"I...umm...I promise I won't do it ever again."

I puffed up my cheeks in anger.

"Plus...it was to make you jealous. I don't like her. I hate her actually but I wanted to make you jealous, that's it", he confessed. "And I think I succeeded in it but I didn't mean to make you cry. That's the last thing I would do."

He squeezed my cheeks making them normal again. "Say something."

I jabbed a finger to his chest. "You. Are. A. Fucking. Asshole!"

"I am sorry. I get angry very easily and you have this habit of getting on my nerves and I just lose it."

He leaned closer and rested his forehead against mine closing his eyes and the tip of our noses touched. "Forgive me, please."

I placed both of my hands on his shoulder and with all my strength, pushed him.

He fell on the bed and I got down from the bed and stomped towards the door to leave the room.

As I was going to open the door, he caught my wrist. "Aeryn. I am sorry."

My palm folded into a fist and without thinking twice, I turned around and punched him on his face.

My hand instantly covered my mouth in shock as a drop of blood trickled down his lip. "Oh My God! Oh My God! I am so sorry. I am so sorry."

He had a poker face as he wiped away the blood from his lip. He didn't say anything, he just turned towards the bathroom but I grabbed his arm.

"Let me see", I said cupping his cheeks.

"It's okay", he replied coldly but I know deep down he is burning with rage.

I took his hand in mine and dragging him made him sit in the edge of the bed. "Wait."

Saying that I dashed to the bathroom and came back with the small first aid kit.

I stood in front of him and grabbing his face, cleaned his lip with a wet cotton ball. All the while I was cleaning his lip, his eyes were focused on my face, staring me intensely making it hard for me to focus on what I was doing.

Once I cleaned it, I gently applied some petroleum jelly on his lips with my finger.

Damn his lips!

They felt so soft, I wanted press my lips to his.

The air inside the room suddenly got thick with sexual tension.

I saw his eyes flickering down to my lips and he leaned closer.

Kiss me. I found myself thinking.

You were angry with him just a minute ago. My conscience said.

Fuck off!

I was done applying the petroleum jelly to his lips and my hand dropped down to his shoulder and his eyes closed as he leaned in even further.

I gulped and my eyes roamed his face before they landed on his jaw where a bruise was forming.

"W-what happened to your jaw?" I broke the silence.

His eyes opened and he leaned back. His voice was rough. "H-huh?"

"Your jaw, it's bruised." I pointed.

He rolled his eyes. "Gareth punched me."

A small gasp escaped my lips. "Why?"

One side of his lips curled up in a slight smirk. "For being an asshole to you."

I bit my lips to stop them from stretching into a smile. "Oh."

He tugged at my arm and I fell down on his lap.

"Am I forgiven?", he whispered in my ear. And then he brushed the tip of his nose under my ear.

I lightly shivered. "Maybe…"

"Maybe?" He buried his nose in the crook of my neck.

"I am sorry I punched you", I apologized.

"I think I deserved it", he said against my neck.

"That you did." I chuckled.

I felt his lips curling up in a smile.

He then slowly lifted me off his lap and placed me down on the bed making me lay down and covered my body with the duvet.

Much to my confusion he wiped away the petroleum jelly from his lips with the back of his palm.

"Why did you wipe it?!"

"I'll apply it again later…"

"So, you didn't like the fact that I applied it and now you want to apply it yourself, huh? Fine! I will never--"

I stopped mid sentence when I felt his lips on my forehead, he let them linger there for a few seconds.

"Goodnight", he mumbled pulling back.

"You...wiped it to...do this...", I said pointing to my forehead.

He shrugged smiling.

"You are weird", I muttered.

"Not more than you."

I pouted sadly at his answer and he chuckled softly then he again pecked my forehead. "Sleep, Aeryn."

He got up and moved to the bathroom and I said, "Do apply it again."

He winked. "I will, wifey."

CHAPTER 15: Dream

Everette's POV:

Once again I found myself waking up next to Aeryn, my wife.

I should get used to it now.

Her face was once again buried in my chest and this time it was she who had her leg wrapped around my hips. And one arm wrapped around my torso.

She seemed to be in a deep sleep.

I gently shook her shoulder. "Aeryn?"

I shook it again. "Aeryn, get up. We need to leave."

She groaned and snuggled closer to me.

I slowly unwrapped her leg from around my waist and proceeded to unwrap her hand from around my torso.

As I lifted her hand, she groaned deeply and firmly wrapped her hand around my neck and buried her face in my neck too.

I again shook her body. "Aeryn!"

She wiggled her face and her lips pressed against the base of my neck.

My breath hitched.

I angled my head to look at her, she was still sleeping, her eyes were closed but she seemed to be dreaming.

When her lips pressed against my neck, it wasn't by mistake, she was unconsciously kissing me.

Her lips trailed up my neck pressing soft kisses. Her mouth slightly parted and she bit my skin gently. I decided not to think about anything else and enjoy this moment knowing she will regret this as soon as she wakes up.

It's okay, she is just kissing my neck.

My hand went around her waist and tightened, my eyes closed as I felt myself getting turned on.

Her lips moved across my jaw but then I was caught off-guard when they landed on my lips.

I pulled my head back and shouted. "Aeryn!"

With a start she woke up and looking down at how she was clinging onto me, she moved back.

I was breathing heavily as I stared at her, her eyes widened. "D-did I do something?"

"What were you dreaming about?", I asked suspiciously.

She opened her mouth to speak but then she realised something and she closed her mouth and chewed on her lips. A blush slowly crept up her neck, reddening her cheeks and the tip of her ears burnt.

"Aeryn, I asked you something."

"N-nothing...", she stuttered.

"What nothing?"

"I-I... don't remember what I was...d-dreaming...", she spoke nervously.

My body hovered hers, I stared into her eyes. "You are lying."

She shook her head. "No."

My eyes narrowed at her. "Were you dreaming about kissing me?"

She gulped, her eyes roaming the room refusing to look at me. "No..."

I pointed to my neck where she gave me a small hickey. "Then what do you mean by this?"

Her eyes widened and she instantly covered her face with her hands in embarrassment. "Please tell me I didn't do it."

"Who else will do it then?"

Her hands still covered her face. "I am so sorry. I don't know how it happened."

At that moment, seeing her so flustered made me laugh.

She removed her hands from her face. "Are you laughing at me?"

"Yes."

She smacked my arm. "You are so bad, Everette. You are making fun of me!"

"I can't help it. I still can't believe you gave me a hickey while sleeping", I argued.

"You were awake; you could have stopped me. I guess you enjoyed it, huh?"

I leaned in and brushed my lips against her ear. "That I did", I whispered huskily.

She gasped. "You are so shameless! Get off me now!"

Chuckling, I rolled off her and she dashed to the bathroom.

This woman is driving me crazy.

...

After getting dressed, I knocked on Carmel's door.

She opened it and said coldly, "Yes?"

I crouched down to her. "I am sorry."

She folded her hands. "Did mama forgive you?"

I nodded quickly. "She did."

She raised a brow at me. "I don't believe you."

To my luck, Aeryn walked out of the room and seeing us she stopped.

"Mama", Carmel said. "Did you forgive him?"

Aeryn glanced at me and then at Carmel and rolled her eyes. "Yes, I did."

"See, I told you", I said to her. "Do you forgive me too?"

She nodded happily and jumped at me engulfing me in a hug. I hugged her back feeling satisfied.

Pulling back she kissed my cheek and in return of that, I kissed her forehead.

Then her gaze fell on my neck. "What happened to your neck?"

I realised she was pointing to the hickey Aeryn gave me and I smirked. "Ask your mother."

Aeryn's eyes widened as Carmel turned to her. "What happened to his neck, mama?"

Aeryn grabbed her hand and dragged her down the corridor ignoring her question.

"But, mama..."

"We are getting late, Carmel", she cut her off.

I followed behind them and went down to the dining hall for the breakfast where everyone was gathering, our family I mean.

Seeing Aeryn, Gareth and Zack came to her and they were talking about something when they all looked at me.

Gareth's gaze lowered from my face and his lips curled up in a smirk.

Putting on a poker face, I took a seat at the table and everyone joined. Aeryn as usual sat beside me.

The breakfast was served soon and everyone silently ate untill uncle said to me, "You and Aeryn left the wedding very early yesterday."

I lied. "Umm...Aeryn wasn't feeling well that's why."

He turned to her. "Are you okay now?"

She nodded. "Yes. Thank you."

We all resumed eating and I glanced at mom who was smiling at me. Actually smiling at both Aeryn and me. And so was Gareth and Zack.

What the hell?

Zack wiggled his eyebrows suggestively and my eyes narrowed at him which made him stop promptly.

And then I realised. Aargh! That hickey!

I felt like banging my head on the table.

It's not what you think happened last night, I wanted to shout but I pressed my lips in a thin line and ignoring everyone's stares, continued eating.

After the breakfast, our luggages were being loaded in the car while we said goodbye to everyone. Mother and father will be staying for a few more days before leaving.

Zack, I assumed was trying not to come near me, so he didn't even hug me goodbye when aunty, uncle did.

So, I decided to say goodbye to him in my way.

After I hugged uncle and aunt goodbye, I saw him side hugging Aeryn and Carmel with his back towards me.

I walked upto him and grabbed both his shoulders. His body froze when I whispered in his ear sarcastically. "Won't you say goodbye to me, brother?"

When he didn't respond, I whispered again. "Run."

And that he did, he ran as I chased him.

Being the coward he is, he again went and hid behind mother. "Aunty, save me!"

"Everette! Stop fighting!", mother scolded.

"I am just saying goodbye to him", I said sweetly.

"He is going to beat me, aunty because I danced with Aeryn yesterday", he complained.

"Everette, you are not going to hurt him", mom said.

"Can't promise."

Gareth walked to us laughing at the situation but when I hissed at him, even he hid behind mother.

"You can't hide forever, Gareth. You are coming with me only on the same flight. Who will save you there?"

He pointed behind me. "That's my saviour."

Aeryn was walking to us and she went and hugged mother and kissed her cheek.

Mother said something to her which I couldn't hear and then she again hugged Zack and fucking kissed his cheek.

I growled but she ignored me and walked past me with Gareth following her closely.

Zack looked so scared. "I didn't do anything this time, brother."

I scoffed. "Of course, you didn't."

I took a step forward and he flinched. Mother warned. "Everette."

"I am not going to hurt him, mother", I promised and everyone knows if I promise something, I would rather die than breaking it.

I wrapped my arms around his back hugging him. I patted his back. "I'll miss you, brother."

He hugged me back. "I'll miss you too, brother."

Smiling, I pulled back and saying one last goodbye to everyone, we all sat in the car.

"I'll miss everyone", Aeryn mumbled sitting beside me.

"Everyone or Zack?", I taunted.

She scowled and elbowed me in my chest making me groan.

I lifted my arms up in surrender. "Just kidding, wifey."

She gritted her teeth. "I hate you!"

"Feelings are mutual, wifey." Saying that, I kissed her cheek.

And Gareth shouted from the front seat. "No PDA!"

"As you say, brother, as you say."

"Mama", Carmel said. "You still didn't tell me what happened to dad's neck."

"Oh, Carmel..." Gareth chuckled. "Don't worry, I will tell you."

"Gareth!" Aeryn warned.

"What? I am just answering her question."

"No need", Aeryn said.

"What's wrong in telling her if an insect bit his neck yesterday?", Gareth said innocently.

And Aeryn face slammed herself.

CHAPTER 16: Heart's Calling

Everette's POV:

"Dad?"

I came back to reality on hearing Carmel's voice. "Y-yes?"

Sitting opposite to me on the dining table, she looked worried. "Are you okay?"

I gave her a small smile. "Of course. Why won't I?"

"But you haven't touched your breakfast for the past five minutes."

I looked down to see a plate of pancakes kept in front of me. "Oh..."

I picked up the fork and knife and cut a piece of the pancake and put it in my mouth.

"Better?", I asked Carmel and she nodded before finishing her own breakfast.

I glanced at Aeryn sitting beside her looking at me with a frown on her face. When I looked at her, she averted her gaze and continued eating.

I took a few more bites of the pancake and got up to leave.

Carmel looked disappointed that I didn't finish my breakfast but didn't say anything.

I was about to leave the house when Aeryn stopped me. "Everette?"

I turned around to her. "Hmm?"

She stood in front of me and scrutinized my face and her hands lifted upto my tie and she fixed it.

"You don't look okay", she said fixing my tie.

"I am alright, Aeryn."

She didn't look convinced. "Oh...okay."

"Bye", she muttered and humming in response, I left for my office.

...

Walking past my personal assistant's desk, I said to him, "Tell Gareth to meet me in my office immediately."

He nodded quickly. "Okay, sir."

I sat inside my office on my chair and placed my head down on the desk.

A few minutes later, my office's door opened and Gareth walked in.

"Brother?"

I lifted my head. "Hmm?"

He sat on the seat opposite to me. "You called?"

"Yeah...um...what about her, Gareth?"

He leaned back, disappointment visible on his face. "No clue."

I sighed deeply. "So, it's Aeryn at last?"

He nodded. "Yes, brother."

Groaning, I placed my head down on the desk.

"You promised, brother", Gareth reminded me.

"I know...I know..."

"I tried, Eve. I tried everything but couldn't find her."

I lifted my head and a drop of tear fell down my eyes.

"Don't cry, Eve", he said softly. "I thought you already got over her."

I wiped away the tear. "I was never over her."

"But you have to now. You and Aeryn are married for three months now and not even once did you guys kiss."

"You have to make efforts now to make this marriage work", he added.

He got up and came to me. Grabbing my head, he rested it on his stomach and gently rubbed circles on my back.

"Just forget her now. I know you have feelings for Aeryn. Just accept it."

"Shut up, Gareth."

"I am telling the truth, brother. You are very possessive of her and everytime you look at her, you smile. I have seen it."

I leaned away from him. "That doesn't mean I have feelings for her."

"So...you don't feel anything for her?"

I shook my head. "No."

"Okay, then..." He walked to the opposite side of the desk and placing his palms over it, leaned closer. "I will get the divorce papers ready. You divorce her and I'll marry her instead."

Involuntarily, I growled. "You will do no such thing."

He mocked. "Why? Can't stand seeing her with someone else?"

I slammed my fist on the desk. "Get out!"

Ignoring me, he continued, "And she is so kind-hearted, so cute, so funny, so beautiful. I won't mind marrying her. At least, I'll treat her like a queen."

I got up and bellowed. "Enough! You think I don't treat her nicely?"

"She deserves to be treated like a queen, brother", he stated. "Take her out on dates, praise her, gift her things, care for her, love her. Make her realise her worth. You made her so self-conscious."

"I said get out!"

"And if I can't marry her then I guess Zack won't have a problem marrying her either. Besides, he really liked--"

In a swift movement, I gripped his collar stopping him from completing his sentence.

"I am not divorcing her. Nor anyone else is going to have her as his wife. She is mine. Mine alone." I gritted.

He smirked. "That's what I am talking about, brother. You love her."

"I don't!"

"Tell me, brother... aren't you happy that I didn't find that girl and now you won't have to divorce Aeryn?"

I removed my hand from his collar and turned my back to him. "Gareth, this is the last time I am saying it. Get out or else I'll kick you out myself."

"Fine. I am going. But very soon, brother you will accept yourself that you are mad in love with her."

I still had my back turned to him and a second later, I heard the door close and I sighed in relief.

...

The clock on my office's wall struck eleven at night and I poured myself another glass of whiskey.

The pineapple yellow colour tiffin box lying on my table accusing me of not finding its owner.

My mind and heart were in chaos. Mind said one thing, heart the another.

Everytime I closed my eyes, Aeryn's face appeared and a small smile involuntarily made its way to my lips.

But then the tiffin box lying in front of me reminded me of the promise I broke. And my smile disappeared.

I gulped down the whiskey from the glass and smashed the glass on the floor in frustration.

Why is everything so fucking confusing?!

Feeling furious at myself, I smashed the whole bottle of whiskey on the floor.

The door of my office burst open and a heavily breathing Gareth barged in.

He looked frantic. His hair was messy. "I have been searching you in the whole city only to find you here. You are not even answering you phone!" He accused.

I leaned back in my chair refusing to say anything.

"Have you seen the time?!" He walked closer to me.

"Aeryn is so worried about you. And here you are sitting and drinking."

Aeryn. Aeryn. Aeryn. She is worried, about me?

"Get up and come with me", he ordered.

"You go, I will come later", I said dryly.

He rolled his eyes. "I am not letting you drive when you are drunk."

His phone rang and he picked it up. "Yes, yes. I found him. He's in the office only." "Yeah, he is coming back, don't worry."

Hanging up the call he gave me a glare. "Come on, Everette! You need to go home."

I frowned when he grabbed my arm and forcefully made me get up and dragged me out of the office.

"Aeryn", I mumbled to myself when he made me sit in the car. "She is crazy. Why did you make me marry her? She irritates me. She gets on my nerve. She angers me. She makes me get jealous over her. She makes me wanna kiss her till she can't remember anything."

Gareth glanced at me. "Then why don't you do it?"

"Do what?"

"Kiss her."

I ran my fingers through my hair. "Everything will get awkward."

"You both are married, brother. There is nothing wrong in kissing your wife."

I sighed. "I don't know..."

The rest of the ride home, no one spoke and all I could think of was Aeryn. Her feistiness, her craziness, her talkative nature, her eyes, her lips that I wanted to taste so badly.

Gareth stopped the car in front of the house and after making sure I safely reached inside, he drove away.

(A/N: If you want then you can play that song now.)

The house was silent and I went and sat on the couch in the living room.

Behind me I heard someone climbing down the stairs. "Everette?"

I didn't turn around cause I knew it was Aeryn.

When she stood in front of me with her hands on her waist, she looked angry, annoyed but when she scrutinized my face, her features softened; her hand dropped from her waist and she sat beside me.

"Eve..." She gently caressed my cheek with her thumb. "What's wrong?"

That's the first time she ever called me Eve.

I shook my head slowly and didn't say anything.

She shifted closer and gently rubbed my arm. "Something is wrong with you, Eve." Concern was written all over her face.

"I am confused", I admitted. About my feelings. I wanted to add.

"About what?"

"Something..." Saying that I shifted even more closer and placed my head on her shoulder wrapping my arm around her body.

Her hand went to my hair as she softly massaged my scalp.

"Is your mind and heart telling you two different things?

"Yes..." I whispered against her neck.

"Then why don't you listen to your heart?"

"I am afraid of the results", I admitted.

"If you keep getting scared of the results then you won't be able to do anything in your life. Sometimes, you gotta take the risk."

I buried my head in her neck. "What if... everything just crumbles apart in the end?"

"Then you pick up the pieces and start again."

I smiled against her neck.

We both were silent for a minute and then she spoke, "What is your heart telling you anyway?"

I lifted my head and stared at her. "My heart is screaming your name. Telling me to gather you in my arms and never let go. To show you your worth. To love you. To make you mine. To kiss you."

Her eyes shone with surprise, her jaw dropped and leaning closer, I closed the gap between us and placed my lips on her. Finally kissing her.

That's what I thought. Nothing happened. I was just staring at her like a fool until she snapped her fingers bringing me back to reality.

"You zoned out", she said.

Humming I again buried my head in her neck.

"Whatever decision you will make, I am sure it will be good. You will be able to make through it. Everything won't crumble apart."

"Only if you are with me", I whispered.

"Eve...", she trailed off not knowing what to say.

I tightened my hold around her, snuggling closer to her. "I need your support, Aeryn. If you will be with me, everything won't crumble apart."

I looked at her already staring at me in confusion. "Will you?"

Her forehead was creased into a frown, I smoothed it with my finger. "Smile, wifey. I don't like seeing you so tensed."

She bit her lips but eventually smiled.

I again asked, "Will you be my support?"

She nodded promptly. "I will."

I smiled. "Thank you."

I then kissed her forehead. "Goodnight, wifey."

And again placed my head on her shoulder.

She kissed the top of my head. "Goodnight, hubby."

CHAPTER 17: Make Me

smirks

Aeryn's POV:

"Mama? Dad?"

Someone shook my shoulder. "Mama, get up."

I slowly opened my eyes, finding my face pressed up against Eve's chest, his hand wrapped around my waist and his chin rested on top of my head.

We were still on the couch.

I carefully removed Eve's hand from around my waist and stood up making sure I don't fall from the couch.

Carmel was looking at us in confusion.

My movements woke him up as he sat up straight, trying to understand what's going on.

He looked towards the window and seeing the morning light he turned to Carmel. "What day is it today?"

"Umm... Saturday", Carmel answered.

He sighed. "Oh, thank God." Having said that, he again laid down on the couch.

Carmel looked between us. "Why were you both sleeping here?"

I scratched my head. "We were... talking last night...and we just fell asleep."

"Oh..."

With his eyes still closed, he asked, "Aeryn, don't you have to go to your restaurant today?"

"Nah...I started with my periods last night. I am taking a break this Saturday and Sunday."

"Great", he muttered. "Wake me up in ten minutes."

"Okay...", I said before walking upstairs to my room to get freshened up.

Once I was freshened up, I went back down in the kitchen where Carmel was taking out some cereals in a bowl.

"Did you wake, Eve?"

She smiled sheepishly. "I forgot."

"Let it be. I'll wake him up."

I went back outside to the living room where he was peacefully sleeping on the couch on his back, one arm over his stomach the other hanging down from the couch.

I crouched down in front of the couch slowly brushed away a strand of hair from his forehead. He looked so cute while sleeping. Not like a jerk that he is.

Will you be my support?

I remembered our conversation from last night and I felt the butterflies dancing in my stomach.

Last night, I thought he was going to kiss me but unfortunately, he didn't.

I cupped his cheek and gently caressed it with my thumb and then leaning down, kissed his cheek lingeringly.

His hand which was hanging down from the couch caught my wrist, his eyes still closed. "Taking advantage of me while I'm sleeping?" His voice was hoarse.

I shut my eyes in embarrassment and a blush spread across my cheeks.

"I was just waking you up", I muttered in a failed attempt to defend my actions.

By now he was looking at me. He smirked. "I like your way of waking up. Why don't you wake me up everyday?"

Rolling my eyes, I got up forgetting that he was still holding my wrist. As I got up, he pulled me down making me land on his chest.

I blushed at our intimate position, his hand snaked around my waist making sure I don't fall. While my palm was pressed against his chest.

His eyes were twinkling with amusement.

I attempted to get up but he held me down. I glanced towards the kitchen hoping Carmel doesn't see us like this.

"W-what are you doing?", I whispered shouted.

He cupped my cheek and bringing my head closer to him, kissed the corner of my mouth making my heart skip a beat.

"Goodmorning, wifey", he whispered against my cheek.

I was red as a tomato by now but I somehow managed to say, "Goodmorning."

He smiled softly and still cupping my cheek he brought my head closer to his. I gulped.

Is he going to kiss me?

He eyes flickered down to my lips as he bit his.

Why this torture? Just kiss me already!

Our lips were inches apart, his eyes fluttered closed, so did mine.

His hot breath fanned my lips as his lips hovered mine.

I decided to end this torture and leaning closer, pressed my--

"Mama, where are the eggs?", Carmel's voice came from the kitchen.

He groaned cursing underneath his breath. "Fuck."

My eyes flew opened and I was about to burst with embarrassment. We both stared into each other's eyes, our lips still hardly apart but the trance was broken.

"Mama!" She called out again.

"C-coming!", I stuttered.

His hand removed from my waist and without looking at him, I ran away from there.

"Why is your face so red?", Carmel questioned when I gave her the eggs.

"Nothing...", I said nervously.

Aargh! We were about to kiss!

Damn you, Carmel!

She was scrutinizing my face and then she said in a low voice. "Did you guys kiss?"

I felt like banging my head on the counter.

"Tell me", she urged.

"We were about to", I said in a disappointed tone.

"Then why didn't you?"

I pouted sadly looking at her. "Because you called me!"

She gasped. "I am so sorry!"

Then she smacked her head. "I am sorry, mama. I didn't know."

I rolled my eyes. "Of course, you didn't."

She grabbed my arm. "Mama, I am sorry."

"It's okay, Carmel. It's not I am dying to kiss him."

"I know you are dying to kiss him", she teased.

"Shut up."

"For how long will you deny it? Accept that you like him. Or maybe love him." She wiggled her eyebrows.

"Two things. First: I don't...I don't like him, okay? Nor do I love him. Second: Do you keep forgetting that I am your mother?! Who talks about all this to her mother?"

She frowned. "You only said you are my friend/mother."

"Yeah...but I am still your mother. I am elder than you!"

"Just by fifteen years."

"Fifteen years is a huge age gap!"

She shrugged her shoulders. "I don't think so."

"By the way", she said changing the topic. "I think dad loves you too."

My heart skipped a beat. "Carmel, shut up."

"It's so obvious, mama. Whenever he looks at you, he smiles. He is in love with you."

He smiles while looking at me?

"Carmel, you better stop reading those stupid romantic stories", I scolded.

She rolled her eyes. "I am just telling you what I saw. If you don't wanna believe it then it's okay."

Ignoring her, I started preparing the breakfast.

He is in love with you.

No, he isn't!

I am not going to give myself false hopes. In the end, you just get disappointed.

I set down three plates of eggs and bacon on the dining table when Eve walked down the stairs.

We three sat down for breakfast, I was silent while Eve and Carmel were talking. I didn't pay much attention to them cause I was lost in my own world.

Carmel's question to Eve snapped me out of my thoughts. "Are you okay now, dad?"

"Yes. Why?"

"You looked sad yesterday. Are you happy now?"

Eve looked at me intensely, a smile forming on his face. "Very."

His gaze made me blush. Carmel looked at me then back at him. "Did I miss something?"

"Finish your breakfast, Carmel", I said diverting the topic.

...

The next day...

"Carmel! Eve! Your most favourite person is here!"

I came out of the kitchen to see Gareth standing near the door and bawling at the top of his lungs.

"They are upstairs", I told him.

He looked surprised to see me. "Shouldn't you be at your restaurant at the moment?"

"Are you not happy to see me?"

"Of course not, dear." He walked closer to me. "I am very happy to be in your graceful presence."

Lifting my arm, he kissed my knuckles and winked.

I placed my hand over my heart. "Thank you, thank you."

"Will you stay for lunch?", I asked.

"Gladly."

I looked over his shoulder, Eve was standing on the stairs looking at us, looking not so pleased.

Gareth followed my gaze and looked behind him and smirked.

Gareth wrapped his arm around my shoulder pulling me closer. "Oh, brother. Your wife's really kind, she asked me to stay for lunch."

"You are not staying here. Get out", he said walking down the stairs.

"He is your brother!", I snapped at Eve.

"He is being an asshole", he told me in a surprisingly calm voice.

"He didn't say or do anything", I argued.

"He already did on Friday."

Gareth's arm was still around my shoulder and Eve looked at it, his jaw clenched.

He growled. "Remove your hand from her!"

"Do you have any problem, Aeryn?", Gareth asked me sweetly referring to his arm around my shoulder.

I shook my head. "No."

By now even Carmel walked down and was looking at us in confusion.

Something flashed across Eve's face on my answer and he looked...hurt?

Gareth winked at me. "Thanks."

Eve's body literally shook with anger, when I looked carefully at his face, tears were forming in the corner of his eyes.

"Eve, are you...are you crying?", I asked.

Gareth instantly removed his hand from my shoulder and stepped closer to him. "Brother...I was just kidding."

He pushed Gareth away. "Fuck off!"

And went past us when Gareth said, "Come on! I was just messing with you. She is like my sister!"

I guess Eve didn't know that Gareth considers me his sister. He already told me this a long time back.

Gareth looked guilty and I gave him a small smile. "I'll handle him. You both go."

Gareth nodded and Carmel and he both went upstairs.

Eve was in the kitchen looking inside the refrigerator, when he heard me coming, he slammed it shut.

"Why are you crying, Eve?", I questioned softly.

His back was towards me. "I am not."

I leaned my back against the wall. "He considers me as his sister. He told me this the day we got married."

"You don't need to get jealous", I added.

At this he turned to me. "I am not jealous."

I scoffed. "It's obvious, Eve."

He walked closer and placed his right palm on the wall, kind of caging me in. "I already told you. You are mine."

"I am not an object."

"You are my wife."

"That doesn't makes me yours. You need to stop being so possessive."

I attempted to move away but he held my shoulder with his other hand, stopping me from moving.

"And you need to stop being so feisty", he said.

I was about to reply but he cleared his throat and said, "I bought you an Audi."

My jaw dropped. "What?!"

"Audi, it's a car--"

"I know what an Audi is! But why did you buy me that?!"

"Because you didn't have a car", he said nonchalantly.

I face slammed myself. "You already have so many cars, Eve. And I was using your BMW, there was no need of buying a new car."

I didn't give him a chance to speak. "Or wait a minute. You had a problem with me driving your car? That's why you bought me a new car, huh?"

"What you are thinking is wrong."

"I can't believe it, Eve! You bought me a fucking Audi!"

"Calm down, Aeryn. It's not a big deal. Consider it a gift."

I ran my hand down my face. "I don't need such expensive gifts!"

"It's wasn't that expensive. I bought you a simple model."

The calmness in his voice made me more angry. "I don't need your money. It's okay if I didn't have a car…"

"You are my wife, Aeryn."

"No, no, no. I don't want your money for God's sake! And now don't say that I am indirectly using your money since you bought my restuarant and blah, blah, blah... don't worry I'll pay you back someday."

This time he raised his voice. "Again you are saying the same thing. You don't need to pay me back! How many times do I have to tell you?"

"No! I will pay you back."

"Shut up, Aeryn."

"No, I won't shut up because you are crazy!"

He rolled his eyes. "Shut your mouth or else I'll do it myself."

I remembered he said the same thing in Australia and feeling a bit confident, I said, "Go on, do it."

His jaw clenched. "Watch what you are saying." He gave me a warning.

"No. Now you make me shut up."

He warned again. "Aeryn."

I mocked. "Go on. What are you afraid of?"

He cursed underneath his breath. "Fuck it."

"I know you will--"

And grabbing the back of my neck, he crushed his lips upon mine.

It took me a few seconds to realise that he is actually kissing me! My first kiss!

And when I did, my eyes fluttered closed on their own. Butterflies exploded in my stomach, my heart skipped several beats.

The kiss was brutal, it felt as if he was punishing me, taking out all his anger on me. It was rough and hard and fast.

My hands automatically wrapped around his neck as I kissed him back and with a groan he pressed his body closer to mine.

He sucked on my bottom lip and thrusted his tongue inside my mouth.

Damn!

He tasted like honey and vanilla. His tongue slid against mine making me moan into the kiss.

Then he slowed down and started kissing me gently and passionately. His tongue traced my lips before tasting the inside of my mouth.

Abruptly we stopped when he heard two loud gasps.

He immediately pulled back and we both turned to the entrance of the kitchen where Gareth and Carmel stood beside each other.

Gareth's one hand covered his eyes and his other covered Carmel's eyes.

"We didn't see anything", he squeaked without removing his hand from his eyes.

Oh God! This is so embarrassing!

Having said that he dragged away Carmel along with him from the kitchen.

I was still breathing heavily and I slowly lifted my gaze to Eve but he refused to look at me. He was looking down at the floor.

I waited for him to say something. But he didn't.

He took a step back and then another and turned and left, leaving me standing there feeling confused, shocked, flustered, and a heart that was beating wildly for him.

Cause I was fucking falling in love with him.

CHAPTER 18: Falling

Aeryn's POV:

I screamed into my pillow for the hundreth time.

I can't believe we kissed!

And I am falling in love with him! Fuck that, I am already in love with him.

After Eve left me standing in the kitchen, a few minutes later I ran back to my room hoping I don't see him again today.

I spent the whole day in my room, Carmel brought me a few things to eat but she made sure to give me a mischievous look before going away.

In the evening, Carmel burst into my room looking worried.

"What is it, Carmel?"

"Mama...dad, left."

"Sorry?"

"He left!"

"Left where?"

"I don't know. He had a bag in his hand and he just went out, I was about to ask him but he was so fast", she explained.

My mouth formed an 'o'.

Did he leave just because of the kiss?

I will fucking kill him if he pushes me away because of it!

Well...I also ignored him.

I picked up my phone and called him but his phone was switched off.

Great!

Next I called Gareth who picked up immediately.

I didn't give him a chance to speak. "Gareth, do you know where Eve went to?"

"Umm...went to? Where?"

"Aargh! That's what I am asking you!"

He said after a pause. "He was supposed to leave for New York tomorrow for a meeting. I guess he went today only."

"Then why is his phone switched off?"

"He must be on the flight."

"Oh...yeah..."

"Don't worry, Aeryn. He isn't leaving you."

"No, it's not that."

He chuckled. "I know exactly what it is."

"Shut up", I snapped. "Goodnight."

"Goodnight!"

I hung up the call and said to Carmel. "He went to New York for a meeting."

"Oh..."

Carmel sat beside me and I kept my head on her shoulder. "You were right."

"I am always right, mama. You need to be specific."

I smacked her arm and chuckled but then I turned serious. "I love him."

She hopped off the bed and jumped up and down. "I knew it! I knew it!"

"You are in love...", she sang. "Mama is in love."

"Oh, stop it!"

She grinned mischievously. "Should I tell dad?"

"No way! Dare you say anything to him!"

"Then you better confess soon...I want a little brother or sister."

My jaw dropped. "Is that why you want me to confess?"

She nodded. "Of course or if you decide to give me a brother or sister even before confessing then that's a different thing." She winked.

"You are not reading anymore romantic stories. Who talks about all this to her mother?", I said in disbelief and covered my face with my hand.

An image of Eve and me in the bed popped up in my mind. Naked. Our legs tangled together.

Oh my goodness! Go away! Go away!

Groaning, I buried my face in the pillow.

Carmel laughed at me and got on the bed. "Can I sleep in your room tonight?"

I lifted my head. "So that you can tease me?"

She chuckled and imitated Gareth's teasing tone. "Oh, mother. You know me so well."

Picking up the pillow, I smacked her with it and she picked up the other pillow, smacking me back.

And that's how we spent our night. Pillow fighting each other.

...

"What do you mean you can't find him, Gareth?!" I yelled. "He can't disappear into thin air!"

Groaning, Gareth laid back down on the couch and picking up a cushion placed it on his face trying to block me out. Carmel sat beside him with a frown on her face.

I paced back and forth. "It has been five days! Five freaking days and no one has any idea where he is. And his phone is also switched off."

"He is in New York only", Gareth mumbled.

"Thank you so much, Gareth for this valuable information", I said sarcastically.

"Do something! How can you be so calm?! He is your brother!"

"I tried everything, Aeryn. It seems as if he doesn't want to be found", he mumbled again against the cushion.

"What if someone kidnapped him? He is so famous, he must have enemies!"

"Everette Wilbrose is not an easy person to kidnap", he stated.

I grabbed the cushion that he had placed on his face and smacked his face with it. "You don't want to find him it seems. What grudge do you have against him now?"

He sat up straight. "Grudge? Why will I have a grudge against him? He is my brother."

I smacked his face again. "Exactly! He is your brother! Find him! You are not doing anything."

He folded his arms. "You think I am not worried? If mother gets to know about this, she will eat me alive."

I hissed. "And before your mother I will eat you alive myself!"

He pouted sadly. "Oh, Aeryn. And I thought you loved me."

"I love him more", I blurted out.

Shit!

His jaw dropped, eyes widened.

"I mean...I...umm...he is..." I tried correcting my slip up but it was too late.

"You love him?!"

He turned to Carmel. "Did you know?"

She nodded.

"And you didn't tell me?!"

She shrugged. "Mama told me to not tell you."

He dramatically placed his hand over his heart. "Best friend, you betrayed me."

I rolled my eyes.

"Mama would have killed me", she defended herself.

"But I am your best friend! How could you not tell me?", he argued.

"Gareth!"

He turned to me gloomily. "What?"

I stepped closer and grabbed his collar and said in a serious, low tone. "If you tell this to Eve, I will personally hunt you down and throw you in a cage full of lions, understood?"

He gulped and nodded quickly and I patted his cheek. "Good."

"Now, find him!", I ordered.

He stood up and grabbed both my shoulders. "Nothing is going to happen to him. Believe me, he is safe wherever he is."

"I just want to talk to him", I whined. "I am the reason he just disappeared." Tears welled up in my eyes.

"Aeryn", Gareth said softly. "Don't feel guilty. He will come back. He won't leave you or Carmel just like this. Besides he has a company to manage."

By now tears rolled down my eyes and Gareth quickly wrapped his hand around my shoulder placing my head on his chest.

"I hate him!"

"I hate him!"

"I hate him so much!"

"Well, you just said a few minutes ago that you love him", Gareth teased.

I pushed him cursing underneath my breath and he chuckled. "I regret telling you my feelings."

"Aww...my dear, Aeryn. Don't say like that. You are hurting me", he drawled.

I rolled my eyes. "You really are an annoying person."

His face grimaced, his lips curled downward. "Okay, fine. I get it. No one loves me."

"No! I didn't mean that!"

"No. I am an annoying person who keeps on troubling other people and there is no one on this earth who loves me." He was dead serious.

Carmel got up and hugged him. "No, uncle. I love you. You are my best friend."

I hugged him from the other side. "I love you too, Gareth. I mean like a brother."

He rolled his eyes. "Of course."

"You are an amazing person, Gareth. And your annoying nature makes you unique", I added.

He grinned. "Thank you, thank you. I was just kidding by the way. I didn't mean all that."

I pulled back and smacked his arm. "Asshole!"

He chuckled. "It's quite fun to see you so panicked."

"I will kill you!"

"Oh, you won't."

"Okay... leave all this. First find him."

"What do you think I am doing for the past four days?"

"Celebrating your brother's disappearance?"

He gave me a blank stare. "We might argue and fight all the time but I love him more than anything else. Don't tell him though."

I raised a brow. "Do you?"

"Yeah, yeah. Unfortunately, I do. We are best friends."

"Best friends?"

"More like frenemies but since childhood, we share each and everything with each other. Even our deepest secrets."

"O-kay... that's great."

"Yes. So, if you think I am not worried about him then you are wrong. I am doing my best. You need to stop worrying."

I nodded. "Sorry."

"It's okay."

...

Next day, Gareth told me, Eve is coming back on Sunday.

I was happy, of course but I was afraid if I will see him, I will burst into tears and jump in his arms telling him how much I missed him and in the end, I will end up confessing my feelings.

So, I decided to avoid him.

I was at my restaurant when Carmel and called and told me that he is home.

I didn't reply anything and hung up the call.

That night, I came home late. The house was tranquil and I ran up to my room praying I don't run into him.

Thankfully, I didn't.

At midnight, I was thirsty like hell and unfortunately, the bottle of water in my room was empty.

Sighing, I got up and walked downstairs to the kitchen and refilled my bottle and had a glass of water.

Just as I closed the bottle's cap, I heard him speak from behind me.

"Someone finally decided to come out of hiding."

CHAPTER 19: I Missed You

Aeryn's POV:

"Someone finally decided to come out of hiding."

My breath hitched.

I am not yet ready to face him.

I didn't turn around, I froze in right there even though I could imagine him leaning against the doorframe with his arms crossed across his chest and a smirk on his face.

His voice alone was enough to make me feel alive. My heart thumped loudly in my chest.

"Miss me, wifey?" He teased.

Miss is not the word I would use, I was dying to see him and he couldn't even bother to call me once.

I gripped the edge of the counter trying to control my emotions.

He said playfully. "No reply? Did you lose your tongue?"

I refused to reply to him.

"Well...it seems you didn't miss me. But I did."

I sucked in a sharp breath. He missed me?

"Your constant blabbering, your feistiness, your efforts to make me jealous and your annoying voice. I missed it." The sincerity in his tone shook me to the core. "I didn't even get to kiss your forehead every night for a whole week."

"Did you really not miss me?"

He sighed. "Still no reply? What happened to the Aeryn I married?"

"You won't even ask where I was?"

"Or am I okay?"

"Or did I have dinner?"

"You won't even shout at me?"

He paused for a moment. "Did you like your new car?"

"Did you use it?"

"Come on, Aeryn", he urged playfully. "Give me a sassy or a sarcastic reply. Tell me you don't need my money."

If I open my mouth, I will cry. It's better to keep my mouth shut.

Go away! I shouted in my mind.

"I know what you are thinking. I am not going to go away unless and until you speak."

His voice turned low and he confessed. "I am dying to hear your voice, Aeryn."

My heart skipped a beat.

No.

I am angry with him.

I finally turned around, there he was leaning his back against the wall, his arms crossed across his chest just like I thought.

I was glaring at him and I moved closer. He uncrossed his arms and stood straight, his eyes following my every movement. For a second his eyes dropped down to my lips before he was staring at my face again.

I didn't stop glaring even when I stood in front of him. Close to him.

I glared at him for another few seconds before I lifted my hand and slapped him. Don't worry, it was not too hard.

His jaw clenched as he placed his palm on his cheek where I slapped him. But, there was no anger in his eyes.

He opened his mouth to speak but instead I grabbed his shirt's collar, pulling his face closer to mine and pressed my lips upon his.

My lips were pressed tightly upon his with a fear that he will push me away any moment.

But he didn't.

Both his hands cupped my cheeks as his lips willingly parted, kissing me back. His lips moved with mine in sync.

His beard tickled my jaw and his fingers tangled with my hair, tilting my head and deepening the kiss.

Our tongues met slowly, and we both fought for dominance before I ran out of breath and let his tongue explore my mouth.

I bit his lower lip making him groan. And his one hand moved lower and gripped my waist and pulled me incredibly closer to him.

Our chests were pressed together, our mouths devouring each other. Everything felt like drowning in an ocean of love and desire.

Running out of breath caused us to pull back. My hands still gripped his collar, his one hand around my waist while the other still in my hair.

Our chests heaving up and down. Our foreheads pressed together.

My eyes refused to meet his. Refused to see rejection in his eyes even though he did kiss me back.

His breath still fanned my lips. His voice was husky. "Why did you slap me?"

I slowly lifted my eyes and our gaze collided. His pupils were dilated.

"Because you disappeared", I rasped.

"Why did you kiss me?"

Cause I love you and I thought you left me.

"Because you disappeared", I repeated my answer.

He didn't reply, his eyes were searching mine, as if trying to find answers in it.

I asked the most dreaded question. "Do you regret it?"

"Regret what?"

I gulped. "Kissing me."

His lips slightly curled up in a smirk. "Not a chance, wifey."

He questioned me back. "Do you?"

I shook my head. "No."

He brushed his lips against mine with a smile. "Good."

I stared at his face for a moment realising how much I missed him. And then I broke down. Fisting his shirt in my palms, I rested my head against his chest as tears fell from my eyes.

"Don't do this ever again", I sobbed. "Don't disappear like this."

His hand which was still around my waist, tightened and the other hand gently stroked my hair. "Did you miss me?"

"More than I should", I cried. "I thought you left me because of that kiss."

"You think I will leave you just because of a kiss?" He breathed into my hair. "There is no force in this universe that can seperate me from you, Aeryn."

I cried harder at his words. "I thought something happened to you. I thought I lost you. You were not answering anyone's call."

"I am sorry, Aeryn. That was very stupid of me. I just wanted some time alone."

Lifting my head I looked at him through the tears. "Some alone time from me?"

He shook his head. "Not you, Aeryn, not you."

I placed my head back in his chest. "Eve..."

"Yes?"

"Just don't do it again or else I'll kill you."

He chuckled softly. "I wouldn't dare."

I sighed feeling satisfied he all of a sudden bent down and lifted me up in his arms in bridal style and I let out a yelp. "Where are you taking me?"

He smiled down at me. "To our room, wifey."

His reply left me baffled. "Ou-our room?"

"Yes, our room, wifey."

"But I had my seperate room and--"

"Do you think after badly missing you for one whole week I will let you sleep in a different room?"

"Okay...", I whispered while I was bubbling with happiness.

He climbed up the stairs with me in his arms and I clutched his neck hoping he won't drop me.

He kicked open the door to his room and set me down on my legs.

Seeing his room, I burst into laughter. "This is your room?"

He scowled. "What's wrong with it?"

I laughed harder and clutched my stomach. "Who the hell has a bathroom like that?"

He folded his arms. "I chose the design."

My laughter subsided slowly. "Of course you did. What if you have an emergency? You have to fucking climb those stairs to go the bathroom."

"I love my room, Aeryn. And offending it means offending me."

I pulled his cheeks. "Aww... someone's getting offended."

His scowl deepened. "Don't pull my cheeks."

I rolled my eyes. "Whatever." And then kissed his both his cheeks.

He grinned. "That's better."

He yawned. "Let's sleep, wifey."

I hummed in response got on the bed and pulled the duvet over me. He joined me, turning his body towards me, our faces were inches apart and we just silently stared at each other.

Lifting his hand he brushed away a strand of hair from my forehead.

"Who was your first kiss?", he asked brushing his knuckles over my cheeks.

I bit my lips. "You."

His mouth slightly parted. "Really?"

I blushed. "Yes."

"And yours?", I asked.

A look of disappointment crossed his face. "A random woman at a bar."

"Oh..."

He ran his finger over my lips. "I'm glad I could be your first kiss...and will be your last."

"Last? How can you be so sure?"

"Because till death do us apart, you are my wife and I your husband."

My eyes twinkled with love. "Thank you."

"Why are you thanking me?"

I shrugged. "Don't know."

He let out a chuckle. "Come closer."

"Why?"

"Cause I want to kiss you."

Gladly, I shifted closer and he slowly kissed me briefly. "Your lips are addicting." He whispered against my lips and then pecked it.

"I missed you so much, Aeryn", he whispered.

"I missed you too, Eve", I whispered back.

He pecked my lips again and then kissed my forehead and pulled me even more closer, wrapping his arm around my waist, cuddling with me. "Goodnight, wifey."

I smiled against his chest. "Goodnight, hubby."

...

I woke up to find Eve on top of me and peppering kisses all over my neck.

"Eve...", I tried to stop him but it came out like a moan.

"Hmm?"

"I...I will get late..."

He lifted his head and he had a frown on his face, he pecked my lips. "Goodmorning, wifey."

"Goodmorning. Now get off. I am getting late."

"You are not going anywhere", he stated.

"What?"

"You are not going anywhere", he said again.

I rolled my eyes. "I heard you the first time, it was a rhetorical question."

"Whatever...", he muttered.

"I need to go to my restaurant."

He rolled off me and laid beside me. "I already called your friend, Harper and told her you won't be able to come today."

"You did what?!"

"I called your friend--"

"Don't repeat it! Don't you understand what a rhetorical question is?!"

He chuckled. "It is fun to see you getting frustrated."

Ignoring his statement, I said. "Why did you say that to Harper?

"Because you are not going to your restaurant today", he said nonchalantly.

I whined. "Stop irritating me! Just tell me why am I not going to the restaurant today?!"

He chuckled again. "Because you are spending this whole day with me."

"And what about you? Don't you have to go to office today?"

He propped himself up by the support of his elbow. "I just came back from New York yesterday. I need a break."

I raised my brow. "Aren't you supposed to be workaholic?"

"Workaholic? Me? Gareth's workaholic, not me. He doesn't even date saying it will distract him from work."

"Then why did you start working the moment we reached our hotel in Australia?"

He smiled sheepishly. "To avoid you."

I pouted angrily and picking up the pillow smacked his face making him laugh.

He again rolled on top of me. "Now, the main thing."

"What?"

He bit his lip. "Will you do me the honour of going on a date with me?"

CHAPTER 20: Brownie

Everette's POV:

I again rolled on top of me. "Now, the main thing."

"What?"

I bit my lip. "Will you do me the honour of going on a date with me?"

Please say yes, please say yes.

Her brows knitted together. "Date?"

"Yeah, date...where you go out and eat and--"

"I know what a date is", she interrupted.

She seemed to be ruminating. "With you?"

I pressed my lips in a thin line. "No. With Zack."

She smirked. "Really? That's awesome! I would love to go on a date with him. He is so cute and--"

"Aeryn", I warned.

Her eyes twinkled with amusement and she chuckled. "Feeling jealous?"

I ignored her question. "Will you go out on a date with me? Everette Wilbrose, your husband?"

"I will have to think about it", she said playfully.

I groaned. "Fine." And I got off her.

I walked up the stairs to my bathroom when she shouted. "Oh my goodness! The bathroom walls are made of glass! That's ridiculous."

I winked at her over my shoulder. "Enjoy the show, wifey."

In a second, her whole face turned red making me laugh while I went inside the bathroom.

From the bathroom I watched her scramble off the room without daring to look up.

After taking a bath, I went down to the kitchen where Aeryn was making breakfast. Carmel already went to school.

I hopped on the counter where I sat and watched her cook effortlessly.

"What would you like to have for breakfast? There are croissant, omelette, bacon..."

"And you?"

"Sorry?"

"Are you not on the menu?" I flirted.

Her face paled when she realised what I meant. She started coughing and I laughed loudly.

"That's sad...you are not on the menu", I drawled.

She stuttered. "Sh-shut up!"

"You are blushing so hard", I pointed out and she blushed harder. "Stop it, Eve."

I hopped down the counter and kissed her cheek. "You look cute when you blush."

"Okay...now...now go away!"

"You still didn't answer my question."

"Which question?"

"For the hundreth time, Aeryn", I groaned. "Will you go on a date with me?"

"Hmm...since you are dying to have a date with me. I will go." She gave me a toothy grin. Pecking her lips I left the kitchen.

...

"My first date in the thirty years of my life, Gareth and you ruined it!" I shouted at him through the call.

"I ruined it?!"

"Who else? I simply asked you to just book that garden and you couldn't even do that!", I accused.

"It's not my mistake that it got booked by someone else."

"Couldn't you have booked it earlier?"

He retorted. "Couldn't you have told me earlier?"

"I asked her out this morning only!"

"So, I also tried booking it the moment you asked me! It's not my mistake."

I ran my fingers through my hair. "What am I supposed to do now? Do something!"

"I don't know. You manage and--wait a minute. I got an idea!"

"It better be good."

I could feel him smirking through the call. "Oh, brother...you will love it."

...

"I thought we were going on a lunch date", Aeryn said folding her arms.

"Umm...we were going but change of plans", I said nervously.

She shrugged. "Okay. No problem."

Then her eyes roamed around the living room. "Why are all the curtains closed today?"

"I was...umm...the sunlight was coming in and I was feeling hot you know." I chuckled sheepishly.

"O-kay..."

Just then Carmel walked in coming home from her school.

Her attention fell on me first. "Dad, why is the garden being--"

"Carmel!", I exclaimed cutting her off.

She was bit startled by it. "Yes?"

"I need to show you something." I grabbed her arm and dragged her away from Aeryn.

Once we were at a safe distance, I explained to her everything and she beamed with happiness and gave me a thumbs up. "Okay. I will help you!"

I kissed her forehead. "Thank you, daughter."

"In return of it, can you buy me a few sketch books and pencils?"

"A few? You can buy a hundred. Just make sure this date doesn't get ruined."

She gave me a salute. "Aye, aye, captain."

I sighed in relief when she went back to Aeryn.

Who knew taking your love on a date would be so daunting?

If anything goes wrong, Gareth is dead.

...

Aeryn knocked on my door. "How long does it take you to get ready?"

"I am coming, wifey. Have patience."

She drummed her fingers against the door. "I am waiting..."

For a second, I stopped breathing.

Then she sang in an annoying voice. "Tick...tok...tick...tok..."

This can't be possible.

Brownie?

I swung open the door, there she was standing all dressed up and she eyed me from head to toe and laughed. "It took you half an hour just to change into a t-shirt and a pair of jeans."

I cupped both her cheeks and stared into her eyes. The same brown eyes, the same feistiness, the same passion for cooking. Could it be that...

There is only one thing that can confirm it now.

"Aeryn, can you please make me a grilled cheese sandwich?" I requested in a desperate tone.

"Why?"

"Please! I am begging you!"

She thought for a moment. "Okay...after we come back, I'll make you a grilled cheese sandwich."

"Thank you", I whispered.

"Can we go now?"

I nodded. "Just a minute."

I went back inside my room and called Gareth. "I need Aeryn's childhood picture."

"Can't you ask her only?"

"Gareth, just do as I say. I need her childhood picture, from twenty years back."

"Twenty years back? Are you trying to say that... Aeryn is the one?"

I took a deep breath. "Yes."

"Oh My God! I told you this earlier also--"

"It's just a wild guess. I am not 100% sure."

"And if it turns out to be true, are you going to love her?"

"I already love her, Gareth."

"You do?!"

"Duh."

"And you didn't tell me?!"

"Stop overreacting and do what I told you to."

"Okay, okay. I'll find it."

"Thanks", I muttered and ended the call.

With a smile on my face, I opened the door and took her hand in mine. "Let's go."

"Where are we going by the way?"

"You'll see."

We went outside and I opened the car's door for her and went and sat in the driver's seat.

Firstly, I blindfolded her. "This is not fair!", she whined.

"It's a surprise, wifey. Have patience."

This is the most ridiculous thing I have ever done in my life.

The things people do for love.

I sighed and revved the engine and drove out. I drove the car randomly in some direction for fifteen minutes and then, drove it back home.

I stepped out and went over to her and opened her door and taking her hand in mine helped her get out.

"Can I remove the blindfold now?"

"No!"

"Okay."

I slowly dragged her along with me to the garden, yeah, the garden at my home.

There in the garden was a huge, not huge actually but kinda medium size conical tent of cream colour set up. From inside it was beautifully decorated with colourful fairy lights hanging from the top and on the sides. Small pots of flowers were placed all around it. A round table in the middle with two chairs, again decorated with flowers.

Overall, it was beautiful and she won't be able to make out that we were at home only.

Once inside that tent, I removed her blindfold and a small gasp left her mouth.

"This is beautiful!" She exclaimed.

I grinned. "Glad you liked it."

"Liked it? I love it!"

Smiling, I guided her to the table and pulled out the chair for her making her sit down and I sat on the other chair.

Her eyes roamed around the tent. "But why is it so enclosed?"

Fuck.

"I...umm...I wanted us to have some privacy..."

"O-kay...and?"

"And?"

"And?"

"And food!" I exclaimed pointing towards the waiter as he entered the tent with the dinner.

She gave me a weird look probably thinking I have gone mad.

I smiled sheepishly and gestured towards the food the waiter had set down.

I served the food in her plate and mine and we ate silently.

The silence started to become uncomfortable so I said, "Look, this is my first date and I have no idea what people actually do on a date."

She smiled. "No problem, Eve. People usually try to know each other. Their likes and dislikes."

I stared at her for a minute not knowing what to ask exactly. Seeing the blank expression on my face she burst out laughing.

"You are so cute", she laughed softly.

My cheeks turned pink. Great. Now I am blushing even.

"Okay, let me ask you something. What's your favourite food?" She asked.

"Grilled cheese sandwich", I answered.

"Why are you so obsessed with it?"

I shrugged. "Don't know."

"What's your favourite food?", I questioned back.

"Aargh! Don't ask me this question. There are a lot of foods that I like. For example, lasagna, pad thai noodles...blah, blah, blah..."

I smiled. "Nice choice."

She grinned and shot another question at me. "One thing you are obsessed with?"

Without any doubt I said, "You."

Her mouth parted in surprise and she pointed at herself. "Me?"

"Yes, wifey."

"But...why?"

"Everything doesn't need to have an explanation."

"But--"

"Next question."

"Okay...describe yourself in three words."

"Businessman, billionaire, handsome", I said cockily with a smirk.

She scowled. "I am not here to listen you boast about yourself."

I chuckled. "Okay, let me try again. Businessman, intelligent--"

"You are still praising yourself", she pointed out.

"I am trying! I don't know how to describe myself!"

"Let it be!"

"Now, you describe yourself."

"Ambivert, exuberant, crazy."

I smirked. "True indeed. You sure are crazy."

She rolled her eyes and this time I decided to ask a question, a serious one though.

"Aeryn, do you want kids?"

"I... already have Carmel."

"No. I mean beside her. Kids...with me?"

She looked at me nervously and chewed on her lips. "Do you want to have kids with me?"

"I would love to, Aeryn", I said truthfully. "I want to make this marriage work, Aeryn. Have kids with you, spend the rest of my life with you."

Tears formed in her eyes. "You are kidding, right?"

"I am dead serious, Aeryn." I love you. I wanted to add.

I got up from my seat and taking her hand in mine made her stand too.

I cupped her cheek wiping away the tears with my thumb. "Do you want it too?"

She nodded as more tears fell from her eyes. "I thought you will be divorcing me and--"

I placed my lips on hers, silencing her. Her breath hitched before she kissed me back passionately and slowly. Her hands held my shoulder for support and I snaked my arm around her waist pulling her closer.

I angled my head and placed my tongue inside her mouth and explored each and every corner of her mouth. My lips trailed down to her jaw and I placed open mouthed kisses all over her jaw.

When I pulled back, her face was flushed, her pupils were dilated and her lungs worked for air as she breathed heavily.

My eyes roamed her before settling on her face again. "Did I tell you how beautiful you are looking tonight?"

"Just tonight?" She teased.

"No, wifey. You always look beautiful but a little extra tonight", I complimented.

She smiled. "Thank you. You are looking good too but just tonight."

I raised my brow. "Just tonight?"

"Yeah...that too just a little bit."

"But I was told that I am hot and sexy", I whispered huskily in her ear.

"And who told you that?"

"My loving fangirls", I stated.

She gave me a tight smile. "Then why don't you go marry one of your fangirls only?"

Shoving me she walked away from me but I caught her wrist and pulled her back making her crash into my chest.

I whispered again in her ear. "I told you, I would rather die than marrying anyone else."

Her eyes twinkled with happiness but she had a poker face on. "Whatever."

I kissed her again. This time just for a few seconds and bit her lip before pulling back.

"Are we going home now?", she asked diverting the topic.

"As you wish, wifey."

She smiled and walked towards the exit when I stopped her. "The blindfold!"

"Why do I need a blindfold now? I already saw your surprise."

Damn you Gareth! What am I supposed do now?!

"I...umm... because...umm..."

She started laughing all of a sudden making me frown and she placed her hand on my shoulder. "Did you really think I would not realise that we are at home only?"

My jaw dropped. "You knew?!"

She rolled her eyes while chuckling. "Duh."

I face slammed myself. "I am sorry."

She removed my hand from my face. "It's okay. I really enjoyed it. But you should have told me this, why did you hide it?"

I sighed. "I just wanted our first date to be perfect and not some simple dinner in our garden only, so..."

"Okay, okay. I get it."

I groaned. "This is so embarrassing!"

She chuckled again. "Can we go now?"

"Yeah, sure."

She held my hand in hers and we walked out through the exit and walked back home.

As we went inside the house she said, "You still want a grilled cheese sandwich?"

How could I forget that?

"Yes, please."

She smiled. "Okay, I'll make it."

"I'll be in the study", I told her and she hummed in response and I went to my study.

Sitting on my chair, I opened the drawer in the desk and pulled out the pineapple yellow colour tiffin box. And sighed.

For the next fifteen minutes, I stared at it lost in my thoughts. There was a knock at the door and I put the tiffin box inside before telling her to come in.

She placed a plate in front of me that had the grilled cheese sandwich and I gulped nervously.

She told me that she is going down to the kitchen and I nodded.

When she went away, I nervously picked up the sandwich, my hand was shaking. This is it. The moment of truth.

My phone rang and seeing Gareth calling, I picked it up and at the same time I took a bite of the sandwich.

"Brother! I found her!"

Tears welled up in my eyes, not because of what he said but because of the taste of the sandwich, the taste I had been searching for the past twenty years.

"Brother?"

"Y-yes?"

"Did you hear what I said?"

I sniffed. "I did." And I ended the call.

I grabbed the tiffin box and ran down the stairs to the kitchen where she was fetching herself a glass of water. Her back was towards me.

"Brownie?" I managed to say in a rough voice. My voice cracking already.

And her body froze.

CHAPTER 21: Back To You

Shit! I should have updated 25 minutes ago . Sorry.

Aeryn's POV:

"Brownie?"

My whole body froze on hearing him call me that.

This can't be possible.

He can't be--

I turned around, Eve was standing there with tears rolling down his eyes. He had my pineapple yellow colour tiffin box in his hand.

Those deep blue eyes.

How the fuck I didn't notice it before?

A small sob left my mouth. Before I knew it, tears were falling down my eyes just like him.

We just stood there, crying and staring at each other not believing if everything is for real or it's just a beautiful dream.

Slowly, he took a hesitant step towards me. His feet wobbling.

My hand covered my mouth trying to control my sobs and his steps faltered.

His hands were shaking when he stood close to me, his eyes focused on the tiffin box.

His voice shook. "Th-this belo-ngs to you. I-I... couldn't give it b-back. Thank you for the sand-wich...it was delicious as always."

He lifted his gaze and looked at me, I was a crying mess. I took the tiffin box from his hand and kept it on the counter behind me and hugged him tightly.

Wrapping my arms around his torso I buried my face in his chest and he hugged me back tightly wrapping his arms around my body and placing his chin on the top of my head.

We both broke down, crying our hearts out.

"My little Brownie", he crooned making me cry harder.

Five minutes passed and we were still standing in the same position, still crying, still hugging and holding each other tightly afraid of letting go.

Hesitantly he pulled apart, just a little bit but I refused to let go of him. He wrapped his arm around my shoulder and with my face still buried in his chest, he walked us to the living room and sitting down on the couch made me sit on his lap and I immediately wrapped my arms around his neck and hid my face in the crook of his neck.

His fingers gently stroked my hair, the other hand around my waist. None of us said a single thing, the silence and the tears spoke for us.

"My little Brownie?" His voice was low and soft and still cracking because of crying.

I lifted my head from his neck and with his hand that was still shaking, he cupped my cheek and rested his forehead against mine and closed his eyes ad tears fell from his eyes.

"I searched for you so hard", he whispered in a rough voice. "You were right beside me all this time yet I couldn't find you."

"I am here now", I whispered.

He pulled back a bit and watched my face through the tears, the tiniest of smile forming on his lips.

I wiped away his tears with my fingers. "You are crying...are you not happy to find me?"

He chuckled and sobbed at the same time. "I have never been this happy."

Wiping away my own tears, I placed my head on his shoulder. "Eve...you left me then. You went away. I was so worried about you."

"I am not leaving you ever again."

I smiled to myself feeling satisfied.

"What happened after you went away? I was so afraid thinking about whether your uncle fulfilled his promise or not."

"What do you think?"

I looked at him. I did meet his uncle, he was sweet. Eve is a billionaire now. It means...

"He fulfilled his promise", I said.

"He did. He promised us a better life and he did give us a better life. He didn't break his promise; he supported us at every point of our life. He was setting up his own company, he was busy with it so he never gave attention to us but he repented it later. So, as soon as his company gained success, the first thing he did was call us to him and he did everything to make up for his mistake." He explained.

"When he fulfilled his promise, it filled me with so much joy that I vowed to myself to never break a promise", he added.

"You promised to marry me", I reminded him.

"And I did. But I never knew who you were exactly."

I lifted my head. "You said no matter which part of the world I am in, I will always find my way back to you."

Smiling he leaned his forehead against mine. "Yes. I found my way back to you."

He kissed my forehead. "It's ironical how everything I promised to you I fulfilled without even knowing who you are exactly."

I sighed. "Why didn't we ever ask each other's name?"

"That was and will remain a mystery."

I trailed my fingers down his face. "I am so proud of what you have become, Eve. You hardly had anything to eat and now...now you are one of the richest person in the world."

He smiled softly. "All thanks to uncle and a little bit of Gareth's and my hardwork."

I chuckled but then a sob escaped my mouth. I still can't believe this.

Seeing me cry, the tears fell from his eyes too. Our eyes fell on each other's lips.

With quivering lips we slowly leaned closer and closer until our lips met making my heart skip a beat.

The tears made the kiss salty as our lips moved leisurely against each other. His fingers held my neck and my fingers tangled in his hair.

His tongue traced my lips asking for entrance which I gave willingly and our tongues danced together.

My hand trailed down his hair onto his neck and down to his chest and under his T-shirt as I slowly traced my fingers over his abs.

With a groan, he got up wrapping my legs around his torso and without removing his lips from me he carried me upstairs.

My lips moved down to his jaw and down to his neck where I pressed kisses all over his neck.

Carrying me to his room he placed me down on the bed before standing in front of me breathing heavily. I was about to protest at the loss of contact but he quickly pulled his T-shirt over his head and throwing it on the floor got on top of me and covered my mouth with his again.

His lips trailed down to my neck where he sucked my skin making me moan. The dress which I wore had an off shoulder which gave him more access to give me hickeys all over my neck and shoulder making my back arch in pleasure.

Then with a groan he pulled back, his hands on either side of my head and his body hovering mine; his eyes a much darker shade of blue.

His voice was low and husky. "Aeryn, do I have your permission?"

He didn't need to ask, I loved and trusted him more than anyone else.

"Yes." I breathed out.

"You sure?"

I nodded quickly and grabbing his face collided my lips with his giving him the permission he needed.

...

I woke up to find my face pressed into Eve's chest and our legs tangled together. The feel of the duvet brushing against our naked body reminded me of last night and I blushed hard.

Eve was still asleep, I shifted my body a bit upward to come face to face with him.

His face looked so relaxed and even though he was asleep, he looked satisfied and at peace.

Leaning closer, I pecked the tip of his nose, then pecked both his cheeks, his forehead, his eyelids, and then his lips.

As I leaned back after pecking his lips, his mouth twisted into a slight smirk.

"That's a nice way of waking me up, brownie", he said with his eyes still closed.

A blush crawled up my neck. "Is it?"

He opened his eyes and pecked my lips. "Yes."

"Are you feeling okay?" He proceeded to ask.

"Yes...a bit tired though."

He smiled mischievously. "That's a sign as to how much you enjoyed last night."

I smacked his arm. "Shut up."

I tried to detach myself from him but he groaned. "Where are you going?"

"Do you keep forgetting I have a restaurant to manage? And you have an office to go to."

He groaned deeply. "Let's take another day off."

"No. I am going to my restaurant and you are going to your office. End of the story."

I found his T shirt on the floor and I wore it, covering my body from his lustful gaze.

"Then you will have to make it up to me tonight", he said as I walked to the door.

"I'll see", I said playfully over my shoulder.

…

I was closing the restaurant when an Aston Martin stopped in front of it.

The door opened and Eve stepped out.

I hung my purse over my shoulder and walked to him. "What are you doing here?"

"I came to pick up my wife", he answered with a grin.

"Your wife already has a car parked over there", I said pointing towards the Audi he bought for me.

"Don't worry. I'll tell my driver to drive it back home. You come with me."

"Okay", I said and sat in the passenger's seat.

Starting the engine he drove away.

"Did Carmel have dinner?", I asked him.

He sighed. "Gareth took her out for movies."

"You are saying as if he took her out on a date."

His face grimaced. "No! In a friendly way of course. As they say, they are best friends."

I chuckled but then realised something. "Movies?! She has school tomorrow!"

He rolled his eyes. "Exactly. That's what I said too but they didn't listen to me. Before I could say anything they both ran away."

I sighed.

A few minutes later he stopped the car at the side of the road. At a distance was an ice cream truck standing.

He gestured to it. "Ice cream?"

I nodded excitedly. "Yes."

"Which flavor, my queen?"

My queen.

"Umm... vanilla."

He nodded and left the car. I watched him from the car buying ice cream from the truck.

A moment later he came back with a double scoop of vanilla in a cone and chocolate for himself.

Before entering the car, he said to me through the window. "Wanna take a walk?"

I smiled. "Sure." He opened the door for me and I stepped out and he handed me the ice cream.

Since it was getting late at night, only a few cars were passing by. We started walking on the footpath, our fingers were intertwined while the other hand held our respective ice creams.

I rested my head against his bicep while licking my ice cream.

"How was your day at work today?", I asked him.

"Boring. And yours?"

"Tiring but fun", I answered.

"If you are tired we can go home", he suggested.

"No. I don't want to."

"As you say."

Soon, our ice creams finished and he stopped walking making me halt to.

He faced me. "I need to show you something."

"Okay...", I trailed off not knowing what to say.

His hand dug to the back pocket of his jeans. And he took out a small rose gold colour jwellery box.

"I bought this ring a few years back hoping one day when I will marry my Brownie, this will be her wedding ring", he explained. "Since now I have found you, I want you to accept this ring."

"Eve...I already have a wedding ring." I lifted my left hand to show him.

He took my hand in his and removed the wedding ring and slid it down my middle finger.

"There", he said. "It's not a wedding ring anymore."

He opened the box and I almost gasped looking at how gorgeous the ring was. "Will you accept it?"

"Yes", I said softly.

He smiled widely and taking out the ring, slid it down my ring finger. He lifted my hand up to his mouth and kissed the ring and then my knuckles.

"I got it designed especially for you", he told me.

I looked at it and then at him. "I love it. It's beautiful."

He stared at me intensely. "Just like you."

I bit my lips to stop myself from smiling like a fool. "Thanks."

Cupping my cheek, he kissed my forehead lingeringly and then pressed his lips upon mine.

CHAPTER 22: Misunderstanding

Aeryn's POV:

"You didn't need to stay with me. You could have gone home", I said to Allen, one of my co workers as I was closing the restaurant.

"It's okay, Aeryn."

Suddenly he took a step closer to me. "Um...Aeryn?"

"Yes?"

"Your marriage is arranged right?"

My mouth parted in surprise. "How do you know that?"

"I heard you talking with Harper the other day."

I panicked. "Allen, you can't tell it to anyone. It shouldn't reach the media."

He gestured with his hands to calm down. "I know, Aeryn. I am not saying it to anyone."

I sighed. "Thank you."

He smiled softly and took another step closer. "I was thinking that since your marriage is arranged...will you go out on a date with me?"

My jaw dropped. "What?"

He stepped more closer and grabbed my forearm. "I know you don't love him. Please, come on a date with me."

I yanked myself out of his grip. "You don't know whether I love him or not. Even if I don't love him, I am still married to him and I don't cheat."

His face inched closer. "You love him?"

"Yes. I love him, Allen. I can't go on a date with you."

He sighed. "Please."

"This is absurd, Allen! I can't go on a date with you!"

"Then a kiss?"

"What?!"

"A kiss, Aeryn. I want to kiss you, just one kiss."

I took a step back but he caught my wrist pulling me closer. "Leave me, Allen."

His face came closer to mine, his lips inches apart. "Just one kiss", he whispered.

I was about to push him away but he placed his lips on mine.

What the fuck!

As his lips touched mine, all of a sudden he was pulled back and my eyes widened to see Eve lifting him by his collar. And then he punched him in his jaw and he fell down.

"Don't dare to touch my wife ever again!", Eve bellowed.

Then he turned to me, eyes blazing with rage. It scared me. He grabbed my bicep and dragged me to his car and shoved me inside.

Sitting in the driver's seat he gripped the steering wheel tightly enough to turn his knuckles white as he drove away.

"All those kisses that we shared, were they not enough?", he spat.

"Eve... it's not what you think..."

"Then what is it, Aeryn?! You think I will tolerate watching you lock lips with others?"

"No! He kissed me! It's not my mistake!"

"It hurts, Aeryn! I can't see you kissing other people while you are married to me. You are my wife! You are mine!"

"Eve...I am sorry!", I said desperately.

"Don't! Just shut up."

I flinched at his tone and decided to be silent. It hurts to see him hurting.

I wanted to tell him how much I love him, that I will never ever look at a man the way I look at him. That no one can make me happy but him. That he is my first love and will always be my last.

He stopped the car in front of the house and didn't even bother turning to me. "Go inside."

"Are you not coming?", I asked unbuckling my seatbelt.

"No", he said coldly.

"But--"

"Go inside, Aeryn."

"Okay", I whispered gloomily and got off the car. I turned around to watch him as he drove away.

Sighing heavily, I went inside the house. He clearly doesn't want to see my face tonight.

With that thought, instead of going to our bedroom, I went to my previous bedroom.

I changed my clothes and stood near the window from where I stared outside. A lightning struck somewhere and it started drizzling. Soon, the drizzle turned into a heavy rainfall.

I hope he comes back soon.

I laid down on the bed and decided to wait for him but since I was so tired, I fell asleep.

...

In the middle of the night, I woke up with a start. I looked out the window, it had stopped raining. Next I checked the time, it was four in the morning.

Throwing away the duvet from me, I sprang up and walked out to check on Eve.

As I reached his room, I cautiously opened his door and peeked inside.

He was there, laid down on the bed but he was whimpering and shivering.

I instantly walked closer to him, his body was literally shivering and whimpers escaped his mouth. I noticed his shirt was wet, not even wet, the whole shirt was drenched and so was his jeans.

I placed my palm over his forehead and he was burning with fever.

What am I supposed to do now?

I saw his phone lying on the nightstand and I picked it up. Thankfully, it didn't have a password.

I quickly dialled Gareth's phone number and he picked up a few seconds later.

"It's still too early to shout at me, brother. I am working on that project, it will take time", he said in a hoarse voice.

"Gareth?"

He paused. "Aeryn?"

"Gareth…E-ve…he has a high fever. And he seems to be unconscious. I don't know what to do. Can you call a doctor?"

"Don't worry, Aeryn. I am coming and so is the doctor."

"Thanks", I mumbled and he ended the call.

I need him to get rid of these wet clothes.

I sighed knowing that I have to change his clothes myself.

You have already seen everything. A voice in my head said and I shut it out before I could blush.

I took out a plain loose t shirt and a pair of sweatpants from his closet and sat down on the bed beside him.

I started unbuttoning his shirt and slowly slid it down his body with much difficulty because he is so heavy. It was difficult to lift up his body.

Since his body was wet, I first dried it with a towel and made him wear the t shirt.

Next, I unbuckled the belt around his waist and slid down his jeans from his legs.

Great! His boxers are wet too.

Duh.

Am I supposed to change his boxers too? I will die of embarrassment.

You weren't feeling embarrassed when you removed his boxers yourself the other day.

Shut up!

I blushed at that memory. I had his permission at that time. Right now he is unconscious and I am invading his privacy.

You are his wife.

That doesn't give me the right to do whatever I want!

Shutting out all the thoughts, I closed my eyes and quickly removed his boxers and made him wear a different one.

I sighed and opened my eyes and drying his legs with the towel finally made him wear the pair of sweatpants.

Done!

He was still whimpering and shivering and I covered him with the duvet before disposing off his wet clothes in the laundry.

I again got on the bed laying beside him, hugged his body while I gently massaged his forehead with one hand.

I hope he will be fine.

I kissed his cheek and whispered in his ear, "I love you, Eve."

A few minutes later, I heard some footsteps and I got up. The door opened and Gareth walked in with a doctor following behind him.

I got off the bed and Gareth gestured me to leave the doctor alone and I went outside with him.

"He will be alright", he said seeing my gloomy face.

I hummed in response and he side hugged me, gently rubbing my arm in assurance.

"He is angry with me", I told him.

"Why?"

So, I told him everything that happened and when I finished, he said, "It's not your mistake, Aeryn. He kissed you."

"I know", I whispered. "I tried to make him understand but he didn't listen to me."

"He is very possessive of you. He tends to get hyper to see you with someone else. I am sure he will realise his mistake", he assured me.

I sighed. "I hope so."

We stood there for some more time before the doctor came out and told us that he will be fine and will wake up later and he suggested me to wipe his body with a wet cloth.

We both thanked him and he went away after which we both went inside the room.

I sat beside Eve on the bed and Gareth was standing near him when he bent down and to my surprise he lightly pecked his forehead. "Get well soon, brother. We still have an important project to work on."

My heart warmed at his action and I smiled.

"Do you want me to stay?", he asked me.

"No. It's okay. Thank you for coming though."

"Nah. It's just I need him for our next project. I needed to make sure he was okay. Nothing else", he defended his actions.

"I know you love him, Gareth. No need to deny it", I told him.

He clicked his tongue. "Whatever."

I chuckled softly and saying goodbye he went away.

I went down to the kitchen and filled a bowl with water and coming back to his room, I took a towel and wetting it, I lifted his t shirt and gently wiped his body and his arms.

After I was done wiping, I kissed his forehead for a few seconds and a tear rolled down my eyes. "Get well soon, Eve. I can't see you like this."

Hugging his torso, I fell asleep beside him.

...

I woke up to feel Eve's fingers in my hair gently massaging my scalp.

"My little Brownie?", he whispered.

Tears formed in the corner of my eyes as I lifted my head from his chest and looked at him. "Eve..."

"I am sorry, Brownie. I overreacted."

I buried my face in the crook of his neck, my arms around his body.

"I am sorry too", I whispered against his neck.

"It was not your mistake."

I kissed his neck. "You scared me last night. You had such a high fever. Why did you not change your clothes? Who sleeps in wet clothes?"

"Sorry. I just took a walk in the rain after which I was so tired, I fell asleep."

I lifted my head from his neck. "Why did you take a walk in the rain?"

He smiled. "It reminded me of when you made me dance with you in the rain, in Australia."

I bit my lips and he looked down at his body. "Who changed my clothes?"

A blush crept up my neck. "I did. I didn't have any other option."

He smirked. "Enjoyed the show, wifey?"

I blushed harder and smacked his arm. "Shut up."

He gently pushed me back making me lay down on my back and he rolled on top off me.

He kissed my forehead, then my cheeks, then the tip of my nose, then my eyes and at last crashed his lips with mine.

My hand went around his neck as I kissed him back passionately.

He parted his mouth and I slipped my tongue inside his mouth as he let me take control.

Our tongues met and I moaned. A deep groan rumbled through his throat which was muffled by my lips.

My toes curled with pleasure, my fingers slipping into his hair. The kiss which started slowly turned rough as I tugged at his hair making him kiss me harder.

His lips moved down placing hot, open mouthed kisses all over my neck.

His hand lifted my t shirt a bit. "Can I?", he spoke huskily against my neck.

"Yes", I whispered.

CHAPTER 23: I Love You

Everette's POV:

Since Aeryn was taking a shower, I went downstairs to the kitchen and I halted all of a sudden seeing Gareth leaning against the kitchen counter, eating cereals in a bowl wearing his office suit.

I raised a brow at him and he grinned. "How are you feeling, brother?"

I gave him a suspicious look. "Better."

He munched on the cereals. "Good. Good."

"Why are you here?"

He put the bowl down. "I just came to see how you are."

I glanced at the clock on the wall. 10 in the morning. "No. Even if I die, you would rather be at office at the moment than being here."

He chuckled nervously. "Oh, brother...I am just making sure you are okay. You know how much I love you."

"And..." I folded mya arms. "You would never admit your love for me."

He opened his mouth to speak but closed it.

I walked closer to him. And he again chuckled nervously and stepped closer. "So what if I never admitted my love for you. I am doing it now. I am changing myself."

"I don't want you to change", I stated.

"Of course, of course..."

I glanced at his tie. "You are nervous."

His brows knitted. "Ner-vous? W-why will I be nervous?"

"Whenever you dress up for office, everything is perfect. But on days you are nervous, your tie gets crooked." I pointed to his tie.

He looked down and immediately fixed it. "I was...um...in a hurry."

"Hurry to go where?"

"To see you", he said lamely.

I rolled my eyes. "I am not buying this excuse. What are you upto?"

"Nothing, brother!", he said instantly and a bit loudly and then smiled sheepishly and said softly. "Nothing. Nothing. Everything is alright."

I went over to the refrigerator. "Speak it or I find about it myself."

Opening the refrigerator, I took out a bottle of water and facing him, opened it and took a sip of it when he spoke suddenly.

"I got someone pregnant."

Immediately, I spitted out all the water in my mouth on his face. "You what?!"

Closing the bottle I kept it back inside before turning to him. His face was grimaced since I spit out all the water on his face but he didn't say anything and picking up the kitchen towel just wiped it quietly.

I grabbed both his shoulders. My jaw was dropped, my eyes were so wide I feared they will pop out of my sockets. "Say it again."

He shut his eyes tightly and rubbed his temples. "I got someone pregnant."

And then I let out a weird, awkward, nervous, I don't what kind of a short laugh. "You are fucking kidding, right?"

He sighed deeply. "Wish I was."

I shook his shoulders. "What did you do?!"

He lowered his gaze. "Sorry."

"Sorry?! Sorry?! A fucking sorry won't fix this and why are you apologising to me?!"

He ran his fingers through his hair. "I don't know."

"Who is she?", I demanded.

He again fucking chuckled nervously. "What will you do by knowing her... it's not--"

"Who is she?!" I bellowed.

He flinched at my tone and gulped. "Harper."

"Okay...Harper...Harper." I paused. Wait a minute. "What the fuck! Harper who?! What's her surname?"

He seemed to be so afraid that he looked as if he would cry. "Collins. Harper Collins. A-aeryn's friend."

Oh. My. God.

"Do you want to get yourself killed?! The fuck did you do?! Didn't you use any protection?"

"I did, brother, I did...it just happened..."

"She is engaged, Gareth! She is fucking engaged! She has a fucking fiance!"

"No! She is not!"

I calmed down a bit. "What?"

"Her engagement broke."

"How?"

"I don't know. She was telling me all this. I don't remember much. I was drunk. She was...drunk." He sighed.

I placed my palm over my forehead. "I'm gonna faint."

He grabbed my shoulder. "Brother, are you okay?"

"Okay?! How can I be okay?! And why does Aeryn didn't tell me about her engagement breaking thing?"

"I remember she said that...she didn't tell Aeryn yet."

"Oh... oh...and when did she tell you about her pregnancy?"

"This morning. In my office. With the ultrasound reports."

"What did you tell her?"

"Does it matter?" He asked nervously.

"Yes!"

"That to deal with it herself. I don't care. Then I left."

My lips pressed into a thin line and I slapped him. Hard.

He didn't say anything and just lowered his gaze. "How can you say that, Gareth?! How can you not care?! It is your child too!"

He kept quiet. "Is this what mother taught us?! To tell the woman who is pregnant with your child to fuck off?!"

How can he?!

"I swear, Gareth. I fucking swear, if something happens to her or the child. You will die by my hands." I stated.

He didn't make an attempt to move or say something.

"Go. What are you waiting for? Go, apologise, tell her you care. Make sure she is okay. She is safe. She is healthy. Just go and find her."

"But--"

"Go!"

He nodded and without looking me in the eyes, left.

I just can't believe it.

How am I supposed to tell all this to Aeryn?

Hey, my brother got your friend pregnant. I hope you don't mind it.

Not in a million years.

I will be dead in seconds then.

Oh God! I feel like crying.

I jumped up a little feeling two arms creeping from behind me and hugging me. I relaxed realising it's Aeryn as she hugged me from behind.

"Why are you so tensed?" She whispered.

"I'm fine, Brownie."

She turned me around and placed her palm over my forehead. "You have a little fever, Eve."

I hummed in response. She had a frown on her face. "And I need to go to the restaurant today."

"You said you will stay..."

She sighed. "I was going to stay but Harper messaged me saying she is not feeling well. So, I need to go."

Of course she is not feeling well.

"Umm...Aeryn?"

"Yes?"

"Harper...she...umm..."

She raised a brow. "Harper what?"

I immediately shook my head. "Nothing. Nothing..."

"Are you okay?"

I smiled tightly. "Yeah, I am absolutely fine."

She kissed my cheek. "Take care. I am going."

She moved past me but I caught her wrist. "You didn't have breakfast."

"I am feeling nauseated today. I don't want to eat anything."

I cupped her cheek and gently caressed it. "Are you okay, Brownie?"

She leaned into my touch and smiled softly. "I'm fine, Eve. I have already taken the medicine. I'll be alright."

"But--"

She cut me off by placing her lips on mine for a few seconds and then moved back. "Bye! See you at night!"

And then she dashed towards the door and I shouted, "If something happens, give me a call, okay? And you better stay away from that guy!"

"Whatever", she shouted while moving out and I sighed.

...

I was in my study, working from home, late in the afternoon. Someone knocked on the door before slowly opening it and Carmel's head popped in.

"You are back", I said glancing at her.

She grinned and came inside closing the door behind her. It was then I noticed the medal hanging around her neck.

I raised a brow at her and she exclaimed throwing her hands up in the air. "I came first in the drawing competition!"

I got up from my chair and hugged her tightly and lifting her up in my arms, swirled her around before putting her down. "Congratulations, daughter!"

She smiled widely. "Thank you, dad."

"What did you draw by the way?"

She grinned. "I sketched you, mama and myself. We were sitting on the couch watching movie while cuddling."

How cute. "Really?"

She nodded happily. "Yes! Everyone loved it! The judges went mad."

I kissed her forehead. "I am proud of you, Carmel."

"Thank you."

"Can I ask you something?", she said.

"Yes?"

She looked nervous. "Do you love mama?"

I paused. I love her. Of course I love her but is it okay to tell Carmel about it? Will she tell all this to Aeryn?

"I won't say anything to mama. I promise", she said seeing my puzzled expression.

I smiled softly. "Yes, Carmel. I love Aeryn. I love her so much, you can't even imagine."

Her face beamed with happiness and she clapped excitedly. "I knew it!"

"Does Aeryn loves me too?"

She frowned and folded her arms. "Why should I tell you? Go, find it yourself."

"Come on", I whined. "Tell me."

"No. You tell mama that you love her and then find it yourself whether she loves you or not."

"What if she doesn't?", I asked gloomily.

She shrugged her shoulders. "She is not going anywhere. If she doesn't love you then you make her fall in love with you. You have a lot of time."

I pouted sadly. "Okay..."

Smiling she kissed my cheek before leaving.

There are two things that are eating me right now.

First. My feelings for Aeryn that I am dying to confess.

And second. Gareth getting Harper pregnant and thinking how Aeryn will react to this.

I sighed. Let's get one thing clear tonight.

...

"Did he came to the restuarant today?", I asked sternly referring to the asshole who tried to kiss her yesterday.

My finger gently caressed her cheek as she laid beside me while we faced each other.

She sighed. "He did."

"You should fire him."

"Eve", she said softly. "He apologized. He told me how much he regretted his actions. I am not firing him but yes, we can't be friends like we were before. He said he liked me, that he had feelings for a long time..."

My jaw clenched. I can't be silent anymore.

"Aeryn", I said intensely in a deep voice.

"Yes?"

"Do you know why I ran away to New York for a week?"

She shook her head. "No. But you said you wanted some alone time."

"Yes. But do you know why I wanted some alone time?"

"No."

I took a deep breath. "To sort out my feelings."

Her mouth parted slightly. She looked unsure. "About whom?"

My hand cupped her cheek. "Of course you. Who else, Brownie?"

"And what did you realise?", she whispered.

I stared into her eyes. "That I love you."

For a few seconds she looked shocked. My heart thumped loudly in my chest waiting for her response.

Then slowly her mouth curved into a small smile. "Oh..."

"Won't you say it back?" My heart already breaking into pieces when she was silent.

"Why will I?"

She doesn't love me.

My mouth fell open. "I thought... you...I-"

I cleared my throat and said gloomily. "Let it be. It's okay if you don't love me."

My hand dropped from her cheek and I retreated it back and closed my eyes trying not to think about it.

She doesn't love me.

With my eyes closed, I heard her giggle and then I felt her hot breath near my ear.

She whispered in my ear. "I love you too, Everette." And placed a kiss under my ear.

I grabbed her waist and pushing her back on the bed, rolled on top of her.

I tickled her lightly making her laugh. "Then why the hell you didn't say anything?"

She laughed. "I was just messing with you."

I stopped tickling her and whispered while staring at her. "I love you so much, Aeryn."

She cupped both my cheeks. "I love you too, Eve."

She pulled my head closer and pressed her lips upon mine kissing me softly.

I pressed my body closer to her and deepened the kiss. Our tongues intertwining and sliding against each other.

Before we get carried away, I needed to say a few more things to her so I pulled away my lips from her making her groan.

I rested my forehead against her, my mind replayed all the memories from twenty years back.

"You stole my heart the moment you fed me. The moment you wiped away my tears with those little fingers of yours, I knew I was whipped. I fell in love with you even though I was not old enough to understand what it was, my heart felt it." A tear rolled down my eye and she brushed it away.

I continued. "After all these years, I only thought of you and no one else. Even when I married you without knowing who you were actually, my heart was still beating for that little girl, my Brownie. Maybe, I was stupid to not realise you both are the same person but my heart wasn't, it started falling for you no matter how much I tried to remind myself that I love someone else."

"I...I--" She pecked my lips making me silent and with tears in her eyes she said, "I love you, Eve. And you love me too. I guess it explains everything. You don't need to say anything else."

I smiled in satisfaction. "It sounds so good when you say I love you."

"If you like it then I can say it a thousand more times." She grinned.

"A bit cheesy, wifey but yeah, I like it", I teased.

I leaned closer and brushed my lips against her. "I love you."

"I love you", she whispered back and captured my lips.

My little Brownie...my first love, my wife, my world. She owns my heart and it could never beat for anyone else.

EPILOGUE

Aeryn's POV:

I woke up feeling a soft pair of lips placing kisses all over my face.

"Eve", I groaned with my eyes still closed. "You are ruining my sleep."

He chuckled deeply. "Don't you want to go to your restaurant today, Brownie?"

I groaned again realising I need to go to my restaurant too and it's going to be a hectic day considering it's Saturday today.

I thought of laying down for a minute more before getting up but that thought vanished when I felt a bile rising up my throat.

Placing my hand over my mouth, I immediately got up and ran up to the bathroom not even caring that I was naked.

These fucking stairs.

Eve ran after me and I emptied the dinner from last night into the toilet as Eve gently rubbed my back while holding back my hair.

When I had emptied everything, I flushed the toilet and risne my mouth at the wash basin and turned to Eve who was scrutinizing my face looking worried.

"What's wrong?", he asked softly brushing a strand of hair behind my ear.

I shook my head. "I don't know..."

"I am calling the doctor", he stated, turning around to leave.

I grabbed his arm. "I'm okay, Eve. Don't need to call the doctor."

"I wasn't asking you. I am calling the doctor, that's it. And you are not going to the restuarant today."

"But, I need to go. Harper is also not well. I need to visit her too."

As I said Harper's name, an unreadable emotion crossed his face but he composed himself quickly. "There must be someone else who can manage it in your absence."

"They can...but..."

"No but. You are not going, that's final. Get freshened up now, I'll call the doctor." Saying that he left the bathroom.

...

The door to the room burst open and Eve barged in seconds later after the doctor left after checking me.

I was laying on the bed on my back and Eve sat down beside me brushing a strand of stray hair from my forehead.

"He refused to tell me what's wrong with you", he said referring to the doctor.

"I asked him to not tell you...", I said softly.

His nose scrunched up and brows furrowed. "Why?"

"Because I wanted to tell you this myself", I said nonchalantly.

He looked so worried. "Is it something serious?"

I nodded. "Very serious."

He lifted up my hand and kissed my palm. "Don't worry, Brownie. You will be fine." He assured me even though he himself didn't look assured.

I chuckled softly making him frown. "Why are you laughing?"

"What do you think is wrong with me?"

He looked confused. "Umm...some serious problem in your stomach?"

"Close."

"Aeryn, enough of all this. Tell me what's wrong", he demanded growing impatient with every second.

Chewing on my lips, I grabbed his arm and placed his palm on my belly.

His expression puzzled even more as he looked at where his palm was and back at me.

"I still have no fucking idea what you are trying to tell me", he said.

"You still don't understand?"

"Of course not! First you vomit in the morning...then the doctor refused to tell me what's wrong with and now you are trying to tell me just by placing my hand over your belly. How am I supposed to know--" He stopped abruptly as he seemed to realise something.

His eyes widened. "A-aeryn...are you..."

He seemed to lost his ability to form words. "P-p... pregnant?!"

I rolled my eyes. "Duh."

He better be happy about this or he is so dead.

He got up and took a few steps back and placed his hand over his mouth.

I sat up straight on the bed and watched him as he removed his hand from his mouth and a dazzling, wide smile formed on his face.

"You are pregnant!", he exclaimed. "Oh my goodness! You are pregnant!"

I laughed softly at his reaction as tears formed in my eyes.

Thank God he is happy or else I would have to attend his funeral.

He came closer and sat on the bed again and grabbed both my shoulders. "You are serious, right?"

"Why will I joke about this?"

At this a tear rolled down his eye and he sobbed. "You are pregnant, Brownie."

I nodded happily. "Yes. I am pregnant, Eve."

He engulfed me in a tight hug wrapping his arms around my body while I wrapped my arms around his neck and placed my head on his shoulder.

With his hands still around my body, he kissed my forehead lingeringly.

"I love you", he mumbled.

I lifted my head and smiled. "I love you too."

And he captured my lips in a slow kiss.

...

I snuggled closer to Eve as we sat on the couch, late in the afternoon watching a movie.

His one arm was around my shoulder and he was not paying attention to the movie saying it was boring so instead he kept placing kisses here and there on my face every few minutes. And in between the kisses, he kept mumbling I love you.

His actions warmed my heart making me wanna cry.

Carmel was not at home, she had gone to her friend's house earlier this morning and we were waiting for her to reach home so that we could tell her about my pregnancy.

Thinking about it makes me feel so excited.

I have a life growing inside me. This feeling is so awesome.

We heard the front door open and Eve switched off the TV as Carmel walked in. "I am home!"

"Yeah, I can see that", I said making Eve chuckle and Carmel scowl.

She came and sat on the couch, in between us and pointed at me. "You didn't go the restaurant today."

"I was not feeling well..."

"Why? What happened?"

I shared an excited glance with Eve and Carmel looked between us baffled.

"Remember you wanted a little brother or sister?", I asked.

"Yes...so?"

"Well", Eve said. "You are going to have a brother or sister soon. Actually in nine months."

Carmel's jaw dropped and eyes widened as she looked down at my belly. "You are pregnant?!"

"Yes!"

She got down from the couch and jumped up in happiness and did a small victory dance.

But then she stopped abruptly and turned to us. "Does that mean you guys confessed already?"

We both looked at each other and Eve answered. "Yes. We did."

She placed her arms on her hips. "And you didn't tell me?"

"We confessed yesterday only, Carmel", I said as my cheeks warmed up.

"Oh...then it's okay." She grinned.

She sat down again in between us, resting her head against Eve's chest.

She sighed. "Thank God you guys confessed or else mama would have eaten my head by constantly telling me how much she loves you."

"She used to say all day, oh I love him so much. He said this to me. He kissed me and blah, blah, blah...", she added.

My face became red with embarrassment.

"Carmel", I hissed. "Shut up. Not another word."

Eve laughed at it and urged her while giving me a mischievous look. "Tell me more, Carmel."

I picked up the cushion and smacked Carmel's head with it. "Dare you say anything else!"

They both laughed at me and huffing angrily, I folded my arms. "I hate you both!"

They both looked at each other and then simultaneously kissed my cheek saying, "Love you too!"

I bit my lips to stop them from smiling. "Whatever..." I smiled eventually making them smile too.

We all sat there in a comfortable silence which I broke by saying. "Carmel, you have your martial arts competition in two days, right?"

Carmel sighed. "Yes...and I am so scared."

"Why are you scared?", Eve asked.

"The one I am supposed to fight, she is so strong...I am so afraid to fight her", she admitted softly.

Eve lifted her head and turned it towards him. "It's okay to be afraid. It's okay to let that fear cause you failure. Because when you fail, you learn. You learn to get up on your own. And when you learn to get up on your own, that's when you become fearless."

Whoah!

"Where did you copy that line from?", I teased.

He rolled his eyes. "I didn't copy it. It's been my mantra since I started building the company with Gareth."

I looked at him in admiration and he said to Carmel. "So what if you lose? No one's judging you. Just do your best. Whatever happens next, will be decided by fate, okay?"

Carmel nodded and he kissed her forehead. After kissing her forehead, he kissed mine whispering, "I love you, guys."

...

"Harper, you don't sound okay...", I said to her over the call.

"I am fine, Aeryn", she assured me for the hundreth time.

"You are not telling me exactly what's wrong with you. You know what, I'll call Dave and ask him myself."

She panicked. "No, no, no! Don't call Dave!"

"Why?"

"Just don't."

"Did you guys have a fight?"

"Yeah...kind of...I'll explain later. Please try to understand."

"Fine! I also wanted to tell you something but now I will tell you taht only when you will tell me. Deal?"

She sighed. "Deal."

"Okay. Take care. Call me if you need anything. Bye."

"Bye, Aeryn." And the call ended.

She is hiding something for sure. I will find it out soon.

Thinking that, I walked out of the room and walked past Eve's study when I heard Gareth's voice.

I decided to meet him, but as I placed my hand on the doorknob, I stopped.

Because I heard Gareth ask Eve. "Did you tell Aeryn yet?"

"Do you want me to get killed?!"

Gareth sighed heavily. "Harper also didn't tell her anything."

Harper?!

I heard Eve slamming his fist on the desk. "I still can't believe you got her pregnant, Gareth!"

What the fuck?!

I slammed open the door and saw Gareth sitting on the chair while Eve was standing there and they both looked at me in shock.

I glared at Gareth in disbelief and marching upto him, grabbed his collar. "You did what?!"

The End.

Milton Keynes UK
Ingram Content Group UK Ltd.
UKHW020333031224
451863UK00012B/525